The Accidental Cougar

Enjoy! ♡ Sommer Marsden 1/14

Sommer Marsden

Enjoy! B. Henson

eXcessica publishing

The Accidental Cougar © April 2014 by Sommer Marsden

All rights reserved under the International and Pan-American Copyright Conventions. No part of this book may be reproduced or transmitted in any form or by any means, electronic or mechanical, including photocopying, recording, or by any information storage and retrieval system, without permission in writing from the publisher.

This is a work of fiction. Names, places, characters and incidents are either the product of the author's imagination or are used fictitiously, and any resemblance to any actual persons, living or dead, organizations, events or locales is entirely coincidental. All sexually active characters in this work are 18 years of age or older.

This book is for sale to ADULT AUDIENCES ONLY. It contains substantial sexually explicit scenes and graphic language which may be considered offensive by some readers. Please store your files where they cannot be access by minors.

Excessica LLC
P.O. Box 127
Alpena, MI 49707

To order additional copies of this book, contact:
books@excessica.com
www.excessica.com

Warning: the unauthorized reproduction or distribution of this copyrighted work is illegal. Criminal copyright infringement, including infringement without monetary gain, is investigated by the FBI and is punishable by up to 5 years in prison and a fine of $250,000.

DEDICATION

For Jim. I love you. Forever and ever. Amen.

CONTENTS

Dedication	v
Acknowledgements	ix
Chapter One	1
Chapter Two	11
Chapter Three	21
Chapter Four	31
Chapter Five	39
Chapter Six	49
Chapter Seven	61
Chapter Eight	73
Chapter Nine	81
Chapter Ten	91
Chapter Eleven	102
Chapter Twelve	109
Chapter Thirteen	117
Chapter Fourteen	125
Chapter Fifteen	131
Chapter Sixteen	143
Chapter Seventeen	151
Chapter Eighteen	157
About The Author	167

ACKNOWLEDGMENTS

Thanks to my fabulous beta readers! Jean Roberta, Angela Hocking, Evelyn Adams, you really helped me get a handle on Charlie and Abby and their newfound attraction. I'm incredibly grateful for your input. XOXO

CHAPTER ONE

I saw him coming. I just wasn't paying attention. My eyes found him, glanced off, and went to my bag again. Cell phone, wallet, lip gloss, book...my usual OCD check upon leaving a store. I glanced up at the young man pinpointed by a stark ray of sun, and looked right into the dark blue of his eyes.

I had no idea who he was. Only that he was tall, dark and handsome. And that wasn't a cop out or a cliché. He *was* tall, dark and handsome. He was also wearing a nametag from the store I'd just exited.

Northern Drug wasn't a big place, and I knew almost everyone who worked there. I'd raised two children and had probably spent at least a year's salary over the years on band aids, ointments, prescriptions, acne creams and sanitary products.

Irving was the pharmacist. When he was out Mary or Darren filled in. There were three women and two men who usually manned the non-pharmacy part of the store. Mr. Tall-dark-and-handsome wasn't one of them.

All of this swirled through my head as he shot me a coy smile—downright flirtatious—and raised a hand in a wave.

I found that my own hand, a mere ghost of itself since I couldn't seem to feel it, raised of its own accord.

I could barely make out his name from my driver's seat. Charles.

"Thank God I'm farsighted, Charles," I muttered but then I realized he'd cocked his head in my direction, catching the fact that I was talking.

He raised his eyebrows and delivered another half-smile. What a half smile it was.

I was a divorced woman, I reminded myself. And old enough to be his mother, probably, I reminded myself further. I didn't like that second part at all.

He raised a hand again, this time in a 'were you talking to me?' gesture and I realized I'd never been very good at charades. I shook my head and waved at him, laughing dramatically so he'd know I found the whole thing funny.

Clearly, I'd misunderstood.

Pat, one of the women who worked almost every weekday, stuck her head out and called out to him. He looked a little crestfallen, it was a pretty cute look on an already cute guy. I got another half wave and then he sauntered toward her, all perfectly fitted jeans, low top Vans and navy pullover.

"And dark, curly hair that's a little too long, let's not forget," I said aloud. "You uber perv."

I started the car and left, hell bent for leather that I'd put Charles-the-young out of my mind. He had to be what? Twenty-three? Twenty-four? Given, I was forty-two he could be my son. Seriously.

What a sad thought that was.

Somehow, I managed to put Charles out of my thoughts. I was painting my new apartment and it occupied all my time, let alone practically crippling my body. I woke up the second day of painting feeling like I'd been trampled by baby elephants. And I only say baby because I'm smart enough to know that if I'd been trampled by adult elephants I'd be dead, not just stiff and sore.

Rose had gone off to her freshman year of college, her twin brother Heath was off in his first year with the Marines. I was suddenly a divorced woman with an empty nest and a penchant for pink wine out of a pink box.

Don't judge me.

Despite the cliché I might present, I was happy enough. Very happy. Nothing says freedom like walking from your bed to your kitchen stark naked but for slouch socks and a mouth guard in the morning. Unless it's cold. If it's cold I'm in a giant oversized sweatshirt robe hybrid thing. And I don't apologize for that either.

I made myself coffee that morning, still partially high on paint fumes, and downed two pain relievers with filtered water. I worry about lead. Then I opened the fridge to see that I was out of milk. And cream. Inspection of my pantry showed I was also out of that horrible powdered supposed-to-be-fake-cream chalky stuff that I keep in case of a dairy emergency or if the zombie apocalypse every actually happens.

I pulled leggings on, a pair of boots and a sweatshirt bearing the logo of my daughter's new college. I pulled one of Heath's abandoned knit beanies down over my crazy dark hair and decided, for some ungodly reason, to walk the two blocks to Northern and buy some milk. They had a small dairy case up front just for desperate locals like me.

The wind was bracing to say the least. I could feel color spotting my cheeks. To be honest, I'd deliberately forgotten all about pretty, strapping Charles and his smile. My one mission was highly leaded coffee with some sugar and milk. I'd read the paper and figured out what I wanted to do with my Saturday. I was still growing accustomed to having full days at my disposal to do with what I wished.

The realization made a nervous little shudder rock my stomach. I was also still growing accustomed to being alone. Redoing my small one-bedroom apartment was only going to last so long. Even if it was the first floor of a ninety year old home. The fixing up would end. And yet, the fact remained, that my new digs made me happy every time I walked through the door to see the high ceilings, French doors and stained glass accents above the door and side windows.

Alone.

The word drifted through my mind and I chewed my lower lip. It didn't really scare me but it did throw me. It made me think about my future from here on out and that could be unnerving.

But anything beat the unhappy union Jack and I had had at the end of our marriage. We loved our kids, we loved each other—always would—but living together and attempting to be wed anymore had started to sour our natural ease with one another. We were no longer suited to be husband and wife. Better to be friends who shared children.

I took a deep steadying breath and pushed my uncertain future out of my mind. A lovely cold Saturday with a house full of organizational tasks and books and music and wine was not the day to fall backwards into despair.

"Suck it up," I whispered and grabbed the cold metal handle. Inside the store, there was a hush. The early hour and the frigid temperatures had put some people off on going out it seemed. I practically had the place to myself.

I found a quart of milk in the case, grabbed a pint of heavy cream as well. When I went to the checkout, no one was there. Which gave me time to peruse the candy. Chocolate covered cherries, my favorite. And a tabloid...a guilty and horrid pleasure I tried to hide from everyone.

They were utter bullshit and I knew it, but god, they were fun to read.

I didn't hear him approach. I didn't hear anything, in fact, until he dragged my milk toward him to scan it and it scratched like nails across the red countertop.

His smile was warm, warmer than the ancient heating in Northern. "Let me guess, a coffee emergency?"

I smiled. My stomach had started to buzz and tingle and I had a brief stab of panic that I might be sick. How horrifying would that be?

Very.

"Yes. Coffee as far as the eye can see but no milk."

I was remembering his double take, his bright eyes, that heart wrenching smile of his. Charles. Young and handsome and engaging. And nice, it turned out.

"Well, at least you're dressed," he laughed.

I felt myself blushing. "I'm sorry?"

"A lot of the locals who run in for milk are still in pajamas. I've only been here about two weeks but I had a woman run through the door in Sponge Bob pajamas and Ugg boots the other day. The day it was snowing." As he spoke his eyes never left me and yet he deftly ran all my items across the scanner.

"How do you know I'm local?" I watched my total flash on the readout and fumbled in my coat pocket for my wallet.

"I was on the loading dock. You didn't pull up in a car." He shrugged and his shoulders, broad and hard with youth, caught my attention.

"I didn't," I confirmed. Not much of a conversationalist when I found myself face to face with a young man so breathtaking. And chatty.

"So, I'm Charlie…Charlie Green," he said, smiling.

I nodded. Then caught myself. His hint. "Oh, I'm Abby Marsh. Sorry. I…um…" My brain went blank and by way of filling it in I stuck out my hand to shake. "Nice to meet you," I said, dumbly.

His grinned widened and my heart kicked hard in my chest like some small animal. I drew in a shuddery breath when his big, warm hand closed over mine. "Nice to meet you, Abby."

"You too, Charles," I said, eyes studying his badge.

"Charlie," he corrected, squeezing my hand.

It was the squeeze that did it. I found that fear was a magnificent motivator. I slipped my hand from his, grabbed my milk in one hand and my cream in the other. "Gotta go!" I chirped. "Coffee pot is on!" Then I beat feet after tossing the pharmacist Irving a wave from the front door. He waved back vigorously.

I slipped just outside the door because there were still slick spots from last week's storm and I wasn't paying attention. I almost went down, righted myself and then hurried on. A big mug of coffee and some painting would fix everything. I'd get past the ridiculous notion that Charlie had been flirting with me and that, imagined or not, I'd been enjoying it.

In the house I pushed the ancient thermostat up two notches and went to doctor up a hot cup of coffee. The Elvis mug called to me and I poured in rich dark brew followed by two sugars and a healthy dollop of the cream. Fuck the milk.

"A hunk-a-hunk-a-caffeinated heaven," I murmured.

Elliot my cat sauntered in, saw that it was coffee and nothing he'd enjoy, and after giving me a slow, green blink, sauntered back out. I couldn't help but sense an air of disgust.

"Sorr-eee," I laughed.

The doorbell rang and I sighed. The only thing I'd shucked was my coat. I still wore the leggings and the beanie and I probably looked like something Elliot had dragged in from the back garden. Which was all mud and shallow snow at the moment.

It could only be one of three people. My mother, my best friend Louise, or a Jehovah's Witness. None of these seemed company I was raring to see.

The bell bonged again, the sound ricocheting around the high ceiling and bare walls of the foyer. "Coming! Coming!" I yelled. The lady who lived above me had a toddler and if the doorbell woke him up, he would make as much noise as a troop of soldiers doing drills above my head.

I pulled open the door without really looking and nearly dropped Elvis and his contents on my feet.

"Charles," I chirped.

"Charlie," he corrected. His grin was crooked as he leaned against the doorjamb holding a small white pharmacy bag. "Hi again, Mrs. Abby Marsh."

What went through my mind at the sight of that smile and the way his grin lit up his handsome face was downright obscene. So much so that I felt my cheeks glow red from the thoughts. "Hi, um…"

He didn't let me go on. Thank God. I felt like I was flapping in the wind. "Irving told me your address. You forgot your chocolate."

My chocolate. I had forgotten it. Probably the first time in forty-two years I'd forgotten chocolate. I took the bag when he offered it, holding it by the corners as if it held explosives.

My eyes felt like they were ping-ponging around in their sockets. I studied fetching Charlie despite my best attempts not to—not to be that salivating older woman admiring his hard form and his bright eyes and his downright arresting youth.

He wore jeans that were just on the verge of skinny jeans. They were a not too dark, not too light wash and he'd cuffed them at the ankles. On anyone else, I think I'd have found the cuffs ridiculous. He had on high-top black Chuck Taylor's—of course he did, right?—and a white tee. No coat.

"No coat!" I said without thinking. It couldn't have been more than thirty degrees and my maternal instinct reared its ugly head. Without thinking, I yanked him inside and shut the door.

Charlie laughed, but I saw him glancing around. Taking in the boxes, the painting equipment, the wall that was half freshly painted navy and half the original ugly pink. "It's a short walk," he said.

"Still—"

Now that he was inside I had no idea what to say or do. I simply stood there, clutching Elvis in one hand, the paper pharmacy bag tucked beneath my arm, probably melting my chocolate.

"So you live here…alone?"

I was hallucinating a hopeful tone in that question. One handsome smile and a double take did not a flirting young man make. And yet, even as I protested to myself, my knees turned a little rubbery. My heart fluttered and I coughed almost violently to regulate it.

"I do. I just moved in after my—" I took a deep breath and then a sip before finishing with as much self-esteem as I could manage. "Divorce."

This time I saw the flash of predator in his blue eyes. It made my stomach feel electric. I clutched the chocolate beneath my arm even harder and had a feeling when he left I'd have a bag full of chocolate goo.

"So you're single." It wasn't a question.

"Divorced."

"Which means single."

"It means...divorced," I said, throwing my shoulders back. "As in used to be married but no longer married."

He laughed softly and my nipples hardened inside my shirt. No bra to hide it, I was sure they were visible to him.

"So...single," he said again.

I sighed. "Yes, I suppose that's what it means."

"So that means if I asked you to go get a coffee with me, or to be less hipster, go get a beer with me, you might?"

"I would not," I said even though I was feeling a bit swimmy in the head.

He cocked his head and somehow it made him even more adorable. And it made his young age even more apparent. Which made me feel like a dirty old woman, to be blunt.

"Why not?" He seemed amused. That was both a turn on and annoying.

"Because you're twelve," I said before I could stop myself. Then I chewed my lip wondering if I'd just offended his youthful manhood.

Instead, he tipped his head back and laughed, showing shiny white teeth and long dark lashes against his cheeks when his eyes drifted shut. Then those eyes were back on me and I found myself wishing I could sit down. I was feeling more than a little stunned with Charlie standing in my apartment with me. Alone.

Charlie turned and opened the door. The light through the stained glass side window caught his sharp profile, turning him aqua and yellow and green for a second. A human work of art.

"I'm twenty-six in case you wanted to know my real age. I haven't been twelve for a while. But even when I was twelve…" his words faded off and he turned to look at me. He looked serious this time. It made me take a deep breath. "I would have known you were a beautiful woman. And at twenty-six I'm free to tell you I'd really like to take you for that coffee or beer, your choice. If you change your mind about me, you know where to find me."

"I…" I shrugged. Shrugged! Because I had no idea what to say. His calm, kind words had stolen my ability to think.

"I work pretty much every day. Day shift. Because I'm young…" he laughed. "And poor."

And then he was gone. Leaving me there in a shaft of colored sunlight with a bag of melting chocolate and Elvis staring at me accusingly.

CHAPTER TWO

Normally, I'd have talked to my best friend Louise about this. Normally, I'd spill my guts and ask for her input. But it felt too surreal for me to discuss it with anyone. Instead, the following day, I went ahead and finished painting the formerly ugly pink room. I turned it into a dark night sky with white wainscoting and white window sills. It worked. The room was large enough to pull off such a dark shade with such a stark accent.

After hours of work where in which I'd been fueled by a pot of coffee and what I was fairly certain was repressed sexual tension, I was exhausted. My mind wandered before I could tame it. Charlie had given me fodder for sexual arousal and then some. I could still shut my eyes and see the flex and play of his muscles beneath his tee. And the leather cuff he wore on his wrist.

What would it be like to have the hand attached to that wrist pinning me to my big, soft bed as he fucked me?

I shook off the thought, cleared my throat as if I had someone around to be embarrassed in front of and surveyed my hard day's labor.

Had I been twenty, I'd have painted stars and swirls on the walls in homage to Van Gogh. I'd always been a wannabe artist with minimal talent but maximum passion.

"I'll leave it as is," I said to myself.

Lunch time had come and gone, and I was ravenous. I took a plate of cheese and grapes to the front porch. Though it was frigid outside, my porch was screened in in the summer, windowed in in the winter. The large panes of glass that encased me shimmered with frost but I flipped on a portable heater and dropped into a Pappasan chair. It had been abandoned by my daughter and I had gleefully claimed it as a porch Zen spot.

I swigged lemonade straight from a bottle, tucked my feet beneath me and watched the meager traffic on my street as I ate. I'd left it quiet. No TV, no radio, no distraction. Plenty of solitude and quiet for me to contemplate my insanity.

"Because it wouldn't be so terribly bad just to say yes to coffee or a beer," I said aloud.

No one argued so I figured I was on to something.

"A single beverage with a young man, who, let's face it, is a good seven years older than Heath, wouldn't be the end of the world."

I bit a bright green grape in half and sucked at the juicy center. It brought Charlie to mind for some reason. But I had a feeling that pretty much everything was going to bring Charlie to mind until I either conceded to a date or made myself stop even considering it.

I flicked my tongue over the slippery bisected section of fruit, and the juicy sweetness coated my tongue. I forced the very tip of my tongue against it and then sucked again. "You're out of practice, Abby," I whispered to myself and then I laughed. When I shut my eyes it was me sucking the very tip of his cock into my mouth. Running my tongue across the silken cap and then nudging that small slit in the top of his cockhead with only the tip of my wet tongue.

Lust and need slammed through me hard enough to make me gasp. I opened my eyes to see the mailman standing at the top step inserting mail into my small ornate mailbox. He looked a little stunned.

I inhaled sharply and nearly inhaled the grape. What a way to choke to death. A victim of a dirty mind.

"Hi, Mike!" I called weakly and waved.

He tossed me a somewhat bewildered wave, shoved my mail in the box fully and turned tail and hurried off.

"Coward," I hissed.

I finished my lunch without any more dirty Mrs. Robinson fantasies. But thoughts of Charlie haunted me through the rest of my Sunday. What would be the harm in a little fling? What would be so bad about bedding a young man who could technically be my son? He wasn't my son. He wasn't my anything. But he could possibly, if I could unclench my ass long enough, be my lover.

My lover. What was so bad?

Right?

*

I did the only thing I could do with the rest of my Sunday. I began painting my bedroom, turning a horrible Robin's-egg blue to a lovely pale sage that was half-green, half-gray. It played tricks on the eye and half the time, when the sunlight poured into my room, it looked green. The other half, when the shadows took over, it looked gray. I liked that it was simultaneously two things at once. Just like I was. I was a mother and worker bee but also, under it all, I was a newly single woman looking to shake up her life just a bit.

Obviously, given that "shake up her life just a bit" mindset, the image and idea of Charlie followed me to work the next day.

I walked around doing my office manager thing. Wearing my nice white blouse and navy blue slacks with beige heels. I had my hair up in a messy but proper kind of bun and I ordered paper, dealt with the coffee delivery people, filled in the weekly schedule for the conference room, stopped two fights among admin assistants and got the accountant all the information she needed, but under it all, was a constant hiss and chatter of attraction.

Unadulterated lust, if you ask me. Which you didn't. But I'm telling you anyway.

I had lust in my heart for Charlie. Enough to give any proper Sunday preacher pause. I had imagined him in a wet tee shirt, fresh out of a spring rain storm. I had pictured him taking my hand and pulling me inside the pharmacy because a sudden freak blizzard was slamming Maryland and I needed to be safe and warm inside…with him. I had imagined, quite intently, given that it was, yes, a masturbatory fantasy, him showing up at the front door and planting one on me because despite my trepidation, he had none and he had to have me.

If you can imagine it, I had imagined it. Fantasies that ranged from him riding in like some clichéd white knight to me marching into the pharmacy, locking the front doors and seducing him on the front counter.

It was about an hour before the end of my day that I sneezed once, twice, three times, and a tall, friendly blonde new to the company named Cathleen said, "You need to get some zinc!"

"Zinc?" I was mostly confused because I'd been busy imagining Charlie, bare chested with the button of his jeans popped open, taking my shirt off. With his teeth. I touched my hot cheeks and hoped she thought it was just from a possible approaching cold instead of filthy dirty sex thoughts.

"Yeah. Sounds like maybe you're flirting with a cold." She stapled a stack of papers and then moved on to an identical set and stapled those. "Zinc will arrest it before it gets too bad and shorten it if you get one." She nodded authoritatively, a firm believer in the power of vitamins, minerals and the like.

"Hunh," I said, thinking. If I went to the pharmacy for zinc there was a very good chance I'd run into Charlie. And zinc was a perfectly logical and firm explanation for being there. I certainly wouldn't be there to see *him*. I would be there to purchase something to arrest cold germs in their tracks.

Excellent excuse. I mean, explanation.

"I'm telling you, it works wonders," Cathleen said.

"I'm sure it does."

I told myself all the way down the elevator, out the front of the building, across the parking lot and into my car that I wouldn't do it. That it was just the stupidest thing I could ever do. But then I'd remember those bright eyes flashing and his parting shot:

I work every day pretty much. Day shift. Because I'm young...And poor.

He was young and poor and we were still currently on the day shift. I could run right over and buy myself some zinc before I went home.

You wouldn't...

"Oh," I said, putting my foot down firmly on the accelerator. "But I would. I have made a decision. It involves a spectacular male specimen of twenty-six and a shot in the dark. I don't want to marry him. I just want to..." I whispered the last part. "Fuck him."

*

He was there. I knew because the moment I walked into the pharmacy, he looked up from behind the counter, pinning me with that gaze, and my stomach leapt about two feet to lodge itself in my throat.

He gave me a nod and grinned. It was a grin that said, flat out, that he *knew* I was actually there to see him. "Ace," he said.

I paused, truly confused. "Ace?"

He stood, dropped his pen onto a stack of what looked like inventory papers and shrugged. The shrug for some reason always did me in. Hugely. The rise and fall of those broad shoulders could bring a grown woman to her knees. I knew because I felt like mine would buckle within the next breath or two.

When had I become a walking hormone? I felt like I was seventeen and in a constant state of arousal, not a forty-something former soccer mom.

"Sorry. It's a family thing. If you're name starts with A in my family, you're ace."

"Ace," I repeated, rolling the word over my tongue. Against all logical odds, this silly little nickname pleased me.

When I looked at Charlie I could tell he knew. It seemed this man could read me like a library book. "What can I do you for, Ace?"

I blushed at that. And he laughed softly. He'd chosen 'do you for' on purpose and we both knew it without doubt.

"I need zinc," I said as calmly and sanely as possible.

"Aisle 4B" he informed me. "Unless you need the ointment. Then that's in aisle 3A with the baby products."

"No!" I blurted. "No ointment. Not for me!" Then I let out a little lunatic laugh that probably cured him of any desire he originally had to take me out for a coffee, beer or even just to see me in public.

Then I scurried off to aisle four with as much grace as I could muster--which wasn't much. I found the zinc. In fact, I found a lot of zinc. Zinc lozenges. Lozenges with zinc in them but other things. Zinc strips, zinc spray and zinc tablets. I stood there, staring, my brain double clutching before I finally realized I didn't *really* need the damn zinc so what did it matter?

"Right!" I laughed softly but a little wildly.

I turned around, clutching my box of plain zinc lozenges and walked face first into Charlie. Today he had on taupe chinos, plaid high-tops, a slouchy beanie and a dark gray pullover.

"My bad," he said, taking my upper arms in his hands and putting me back a step. "You okay, Ace?"

"Yes. Abby," I reminded him, even though I liked the name. "But Ace is...yes," I said finally, wondering at what point my tongue would stop getting tangled up around him. "I'm fine. Sorry. I wasn't looking."

How could I drink a beer with him? My tongue was constantly tripping over itself, I'd end up dribbling it all over. And yes, I had decided on beer because putting any more caffeine into my already Charlie-super-charged nerves would probably result in cardiac arrest.

I was too old for this. But that was just the thing. I didn't want to be too old for *anything*. Not even this hyper, crazed, borderline manic feeling I had going on. I wanted to feel this. All of this and then some. I was starting over in a whole new scenario in life. My kids were gone, moving slowly but surely to starting their own independent lives. Jack was gone, dating some proper prim church going secretary of all things. And I was…here. Buying zinc I didn't need to flirt with a guy I clearly wanted.

"I'll ring you up," he said. "I'm getting ready to leave myself."

"Oh," I said stupidly following him. And yes, watching his tight little ass in those nicely fitting pants.

He took the zinc, scanned it, scanned a card and gave me a total.

"Too low," I said.

"What?"

"Too low. The price. Must be an error."

"I gave you my discount," he said, smiling.

That smile went right to the soft wetness at the center of me. It made my stomach flex and my heart pick up speed. "Oh, I…"

"It's how I woo the ladies," he said.

I barked out a laugh at that. He'd gotten me. It seemed Charlie not only triggered my pervert button but my funny bone too. "Ah, charming. How can they resist?"

"Exactly. Which is why now that I have saved you 35% off the top of your zinc purchase, I'm going to ask if I can walk you home."

"I drove."

He frowned. "Damn. Foiled again."

"But can I give you a ride?"

"I'm about fifteen minutes away,' he said, but his blue eyes had grown grayer with interest.

"I don't mind," I said, finding I meant it.

"Thanks. I do have a car, mind you." He held up a hand before I could speak. "But I'm so close and gas being what it is and well, I do dig the green thing. I like walking, anyway. It's a fairly nice area."

I found myself nodding. "I agree. That's why the new apartment."

He put his hand on mine. It was a fleeting touch, very innocent, right on top of the counter where everyone could see. But it seemed to set off fire deep in the secret slumbering places inside me. Places that hadn't felt anything close to excitement in a while. Not even when scoping out real estate and settling on my lovely apartment.

"I'll be right back," he said, staring at our hands for a second. Then he moved his off mine and hurried off. "Have to clock out," he said over his shoulder. Then he tossed me another smile and I literally felt my pussy flex with want. It was like he had a direct line to my naughty bits.

"Oh trouble," I said to myself. "So, so much trouble."

But what was life without a little trouble now and again?

True story.

CHAPTER THREE

He came out wearing a pale denim jacket with shearling lining. I hadn't seen those things since the 80s when I'd actually worn one. I did a double take and he caught me.

"Sweet, right? I found it at this thrift store that opened just a few blocks from my place. I think my dad wore one of these when I was a kid."

I did a quick mental tally. If he was twenty-six he was born in 1988 which was…

"Shit," I said aloud.

"What's wrong?" He grabbed a bag of chips and a two liter of soda as we headed up front.

"I just realized that you were born the year before I graduated." I suddenly felt less sexy older woman and more of a creepy aged predator.

"So?" He went to the counter and I saw that Pat was working. I waved to her. She looked at me and then at Charlie and gave me a grin. She was only a few years younger than me.

I couldn't look directly at her and was having vivid fantasies about bursting into flames or the floor opening up and swallowing me whole.

What is wrong with you? He's a grown man, not a child. He's young but he's obviously smart and honest. Who are you to question his attraction to you?

The thought startled me and I pushed my lips together as he paid her for his snack and turned to me. When he looped his arm through mine I felt my body go rigid. "You're an ageist," he said in my ear as he led me out of the store.

I put the brakes on in the foyer. It was chilly but there was still heat blowing down from the overhead vents. Charlie looked down at me, his slouchy beanie at the perfect angle on his head to accent how damn pretty he was.

"I am not an ageist!" I hissed. "I'm just a little thrown…is all. I'm…out of practice," I finished weakly.

"Surely men have flirted with you even when you were married." He led me out into the whipping wind. Small wet snowflakes were beginning to dot the pavement.

"I guess. I mean, yes, once or twice. But you are—"

He turned to me, his face suddenly serious in the stark white light from the streetlamps that lit the parking lot. "Please don't tell me I'm not a man, Ace."

I bit my tongue. Had I been about to say that?

"Oh, I wouldn't. I mean, I know you are. Just to me you're so…new," I said, smiling. I felt almost sad. "You're so new and your life is stretched out before you. You have all this stuff to do and experience and live. You have lots of marrow to suck up." I clicked the button on my key fob to unlock the door.

"And your marrow has dried up?" he asked me over the hood of the car.

"What? No! I have plenty of marrow! I just meant..."

"Well, that's how you're making it sound." He opened the door and climbed in. We both shut our doors in unison. He set his chips and soda on the floor and turned to me. "Did it ever occur you, Abby, that I might be your marrow?"

Before I could react or answer, he tucked his palm behind my head and pulled me to him. His mouth was warm and soft. His tongue tasted of the sweet coffee he must have been drinking at work.

I kissed him back. For all I was worth. For every thing I'd once thought I would do but hadn't. For every dream I hadn't given a shot. For every wish I'd let drift off into the ether. I kissed Charlie for every single one of those and all the fresh ones I still wanted to give a shot. I kissed him because in that moment in time, he was my fucking marrow.

And he was so much smarter than I'd ever even considered.

His fingers slid along my scalp, sifted through my hair. He kissed me deeper, his tongue hot against mine. He paused to push his face to my hair and inhale deeply. My stomach felt like it dropped a foot.

"You smell really good, Ace."

"Thank you," I whispered.

"Now was that so terrible?"

"No."

He chuckled in the cold darkness of my car. "Good to know it wasn't terrible."

I couldn't bring myself to say anything beyond, "Do it again. Please. Do it again." I didn't recognize my voice as my own. There was so much life in it. A husky, smoky kind of want that resonated through the silence.

He pulled me to him again and teased me with the softest

kiss I'd ever received. For a moment I wasn't sure he was actually toughing his lips to mine but then he pressed his mouth to mine a bit firmer and I felt a shuddery little breath shake through me.

His tongue was gentle but insistent and I relaxed into the kiss.

"And that?"

"Far from terrible," I sighed. I started the car and tried to regulate my breathing. I could feel him watching me.

Charlie put his hand on my leg. "Are you okay?"

"I am." I put the car in drive and backed out of the spot. My hands were shaking.

"Are you sure? I thought you said that wasn't so terrible."

"It was amazing," I confessed, feeling heat in my cheeks at how eager I sounded.

He squeezed my thigh. "Then what? What is it? I can tell something's wrong."

I turned to look at him. We were sitting, unmoving, in the parking lot. "I just realized that's the first kiss I've had from a man who wasn't Jack in twenty years."

He whistled.

"Yeah, right!" I said.

"Was it good, then?"

I rested my head against the steering wheel, resisting the urge to bang it instead. "God, yes. It was fucking amazing."

"Good," he said softly. "I can relax then."

"Which way?" I asked.

"Turn right," he said. "It's not too far. And on the way, you can figure out if you want to come in for that beer. Or coffee. Or coffee then beer," he said.

"If you give me coffee I might levitate." The street lights threw stark blobs of white light on us. When I turned into traffic the streaks across our dark figures turned yellow. The sleet was turning to a fluffier snow.

"One decaf and then a local beer. I have a friend who brews."

A hipster. I was considering a date with a hipster. That's what he was, wasn't he?

"You don't like beer?" he asked, taking my silence as a negative.

"Are you a hipster?" I blurted instead of answering.

Charlie laughed at that. He patted my leg. "Still trying to slap a label on me, Ace?"

I was. That was exactly what I was doing. It would make me feel better if I could put a label on him that made him easier to deal with. How terribly narrow minded of me.

"I like beer," I sighed. "But I prefer wine. Because I'm old," I snorted.

"Ah, I have a friend who does wine. She makes what she likes to call what-just-happened Merlot."

I laughed. "Sounds good. I'll take a glass or six."

"Do I make you nervous?"

We zipped down the road, somehow managing to hit every green light. My heart rate picked up because I realized it would get us to his apartment faster. And what did *that* mean?

"Yes. You do."

"Why?" Again his fingers danced up and down my thigh. They whispered over my dark work pants. I took in his chinos, his high-tops, his slouched hats. Sitting next to each other in my car I looked like his mother giving him a ride home. I cringed and he caught it.

"Why? And what was that?"

"This is silly," I said, finally, thankfully hitting a red light. "I'm very flattered but you and I...we don't jibe. We don't make sense."

His face grew serious. It was odd because pretty much every time I'd seen Charlie, his full lips had been curved into some semblance of a smile. "Take the next right," he said. "Opal Court. I'm the third house on the left."

That was all he said and a pit blossomed in my stomach. I'd hurt him. And pissed him off, too, it seemed. Which hadn't been my intention. But my god, he had to see how ridiculous this was, didn't he? Even a coffee, even a beer, even a kiss...just insane.

I followed his directions and found the porch light to be on at his home. "Apartment?" I asked, seeing the big old house.

He nodded. "First floor is all me. Big place, like yours. Mine's not as nice," he chuckled. "But I'm willing to wager my rent's not as expensive as your rent either."

"Charlie—"

He turned to me, his expression fierce and intent. A kind of belief shining in his eyes I only associated with the very young. "Give me a chance, Abby."

"I did," I said, smiling. "It's just—"

"You're too stubborn to see beyond your fears?" He cocked an eyebrow at me.

"No, I was going to say, I'm much more set in my ways than you. I'd rather go home after work and have a glass of wine and read a book and putter in my place then go out and party."

"So you think I'm going out to party?"

"You know what I mean."

"Yes, I know that you'd rather write me off before you've

even given me a chance." Before I could answer him he cupped the back of my head, leaned across from his seat and kissed me. This kiss made the kiss at the pharmacy look like a peck on the cheek. Every stroke of his tongue, every brush of his lips lit me up like a firecracker. His fingers tickled through my hair, tugging softly at the wavy locks so that arousal and fire flared in my belly and lower. His mouth took mine, bullying me with a kiss like none I'd ever had. Passion and want and a hint of anger were present in that kiss and I found myself breathless, wanting more.

When his fingers slipped softly along my side, tickling but flaring pleasure as they went, I let them. When his hand slipped down from the back of my head to cradle the nape of my neck, raising the fine hairs there so I felt my equilibrium falter, I welcomed it. And when his hand, foreign but strong and welcome, cupped my breast beneath my coat but over my silk blouse, I reveled in it.

My hand drifted down his belly. It was warm and flat and hard. He felt good beneath my fingertips. Charlie took my hand, never breaking the kiss, and put it on his lap. His cock was blissfully hard in his pants. I squeezed, joyous at what I felt beneath my hand. The size and length and imagined heft of that cock was enough to bring my nipples to needy little peaks.

Inside me, my heart and my soul cheered at my bravery and my body raced with arousal I hadn't felt in a very long time. I shifted in my seat, both provoking arousal and noticing how wet I was. How swollen I felt. How desperately ready I was just from a very thorough, honest kiss from Charlie.

When he pulled back I found myself chasing him with my mouth. The car ran, the heat blasted and according to my clock we'd been making out like sex-crazed teenagers for over seven minutes.

It seemed like seven seconds.

"Give me a chance, Ace," he said.

"I—" I shut my mouth with an audible snap and simply nodded.

He grinned again and I had to fight the urge to crawl across to his seat and plant myself in his lap. Already I was wondering what he'd look like out of his pants. Out of his shirt. Naked and over me.

"Give me your phone," he said.

I blinked.

When he held his hand out, my brain kicked into gear and I dug through my purse and handed over my phone. Within seconds he was handing it back. "I'm in there. Under Charlie. Call me. I'll take you out. Or we can just stay in and drink some wine or beer made by strange people."

I barked laughter and then quickly slapped a hand over my mouth. Snow was covering my windshield, blotting us from the world.

He gave me one more kiss, chaste this time, which somehow made it wickedly hot. Then he opened the door and got out. He leaned back in and grinned at me. "I think I could be good for you, Ace. And I know you could be good for me. You just have to stop worrying about everything else and your precious labels and give me a chance. I mean, honestly, what harm can come from giving me a chance?"

I had no answer. I stared dumbly, my body still hot and restless from the kissing. He shut the door and I watched him walk through the snow to his door. Once he was in and the porch light was extinguished, I drove off down Opal Court. It was a short drive home.

At home, I didn't even bother to hit the foyer light. I dropped my purse and my work bag, stumbled to the rocking chair, parted my coat, unzipped my pants and slipped my hand down into my panties. My fingers knew just where to go. The tips rolling roughly over my engorged clit. I slipped my hand back further, arching my back, pushing two fingers deep in my pussy. My palm ground against my clitoris as I kept my eye shut against invading streetlight. I pictured him in my head. Gorgeous and dark haired, laughing eyes and plump lips, big hands and broad shoulders. And on top of it all…kissing me. With that sinful mouth.

Kissing me and touching me and asking me to reconsider. So gorgeous and so tall and so nice and…

I came, my fingers allowing my mind to focus on the fantasy while they did what needed to be done. I bit my lower lip, stifling my cries even though I was alone.

A smaller sweet spasm hit me and I gave myself over to it. Relishing it until it passed fully.

Alone, I thought.

I was alone. I had been alone for about a year but moving out of the house and into the apartment had somehow sealed the deal and made it real.

"Alone," I whispered, standing on wobbly legs. Putting myself back together.

I went into the small powder room off the foyer and washed my hands, splashing my face with water. I stared at myself in the mirror. Yes, forty-two. Yes, some small lines beginning around my eyes. Yes, a little bit of that marionette mouth thing going on. But then I attempted, as hard as it was, to see myself as Charlie might see me.

Shoulder length dark hair with just a few fetching (I liked to think) strands of sterling silver. Not gray, thank you, *sterling*. That made me laugh. And when I laughed I saw the happy face of Abby Marsh. I saw how my blue-green eyes lit up and my face lightened and then I saw it. What Charlie saw.

"So maybe you will give him a chance," I told the woman in the mirror. "It's not like you're getting engaged, for Pete's sake. It's a date." Then I grew serious. "But Jesus, it's been like a thousand years since you got laid. Seriously, Ace," I said to my reflection, using his nickname for me. "It's been a long time."

That triggered a waterfall of nerves in my gut.

The doorbell gonged and for a moment my heart skittered and my stomach dropped because I thought it might be him. *Hoped* it might be him.

It was Louise. At seeing my best friend for the last twenty years standing there, my no-sex-in-a-thousand-years fear reared its ugly head all over again. I opened the door wide for her and then blurted, "Jesus, Louise, what if my hymen's grown back or something!"

She froze, half in the door, half on the porch and said, "Hello, to you too, Abby! Christ!"

CHAPTER FOUR

"I thought you might like some dinner," she said, spreading the Chinese takeout across my tiny dining room table. "I had no idea we'd be discussing reanimated hymens."

I choked on my sip of wine and then proceeded to spill my guts. All the way from the Friday afternoon double take and flirty smile up to his visit to my house with chocolate and ending with the groping in my car. The hot-hot, beyond sexy, couldn't get it out of my head kissing and groping.

I sighed.

"Back it down girlfriend. I don't need you going off the deep end and dry humping the bannister."

I snorted. "But honestly, it'll never work-- right?"

Louise shrugged. Her long hair had been dyed, I noticed, to the shade of a brand new copper penny. Last week it had been chocolate brown. The month before a punky bleach blond. My best friend was a chameleon. Always had been.

"Sounds like you don't want it to," she said to me. She chomped down on a piece of General Tsao's and studied me with her bright green gaze. "You're scared."

"I am not!" Somehow I managed to swallow my Lo Mein noodles.

"Sweetheart, I have been reading you like a book since we were younger than lover boy. You're scared. And of what? Getting laid? Good sex? Good company?" She chuckled. "I mean sure, he's young, but from what you describe he's also smart and funny and nice. What's to be afraid of?"

"Maybe he's too smart and too funny and too nice," I mumbled, my heart plummeting.

"No such thing. You're just making excuses."

I stared at her, open mouthed. Why was she doing this to me?

"Shut your mouth, you'll draw flies," she laughed.

I groaned but shut my mouth. Then I proceeded to fill it with cheap Cabernet and another bite of noodles. "The man kissed so that…so that my whole body flexed. I mean every part of me wanted him. My lips, my belly, my toes…and trust me, all the girl bits in between."

"Then go for it. I do not see the dilemma here."

The phone began to ring. I stood but said over my shoulder, "The dilemma is I am old enough to be—"

"Yeah, yeah, his mother. Whatever! You're not his mother so stop worrying about that shit. Let his own mother worry about him hooking up with an older woman. You just worry about his penis."

"Louise!" Then: "Hush, it's Rose calling from school." I picked up and plastered a fake smile on my face as if Rose could see me. "Honey! How are you?"

"Hey, Ma, I'm good. How are you?"

"I'm good? You?" I rolled my eyed. I was repeating myself because I was nervous.

Before she could answer Louise yelled, "Hey, Rosie, your mom's got a young stud."

Rose paused. I could hear her breathing. I covered the receiver and hissed at Louise. "You, are cut off!"

She raised her glass to me. "I've only had half a glass, baby. But if you really want some insight into this thing, go with the opinion of someone closer to his age."

I noticed my hands were shaking. I did my best to still them but failed as Rose said, "Ma?"

"What?"

"Is that true?" Then she giggled.

"Don't listen to Louise," I sighed.

"So it's not true." She was baiting me. My daughter was the logical, argumentative one in the family. She would get this out of me one way or the other, there was no doubt.

And I hated lying to my kids. So I said "I don't *have* anyone."

"Are you *seeing* a younger guy?" Oh she knew me so well. How I had a thing about lying so I found a way to make untruths not so untruthful by telling a half truth.

"I'm not *seeing him*," I said.

"Hmm," Rose said. Then: "Are you *thinking about* seeing him?"

"Damn it!" I said.

"Mom!" She was laughing, damn her. "You're a cougar."

"I am not. Cougars are predators."

"They don't call them fluffy bunnies, Ma."

"But I'm not a predator! I didn't stalk him. He's stalking me." I caught myself. "Well, not stalking me creepy like. But like an animal. Well, not like an animal!" I blurted, getting frustrated with myself.

Louise was at the table, head down on her elbow, laughing her ass off.

"Okay, so you're an accidental cougar," Rose amended.

"Yes, Rose," I seethed. "I'm an *accidental cougar*."

This made Louise shriek with laughter. I frowned at her and the receiver. "You people are not helping me at all," I said.

They both stopped laughing. "Oh, Ma," Rose said into the receiver.

"Honey," Louise said from the table.

And nearly in unison the youngest woman in my life and my oldest friend said, "Go for it."

I wanted to cry from frustration. Instead, I started to laugh.

"Screw you both," I said, but I didn't mean it. I was going to just go with the consensus. I'd give it a shot.

That night, three glasses of wine and one pint of Lo Mein in me I hit the contact on my phone that said "Charlie".

He picked up on the third ring. "Ace," he said.

"I'll do it," I said.

"And what is that?"

I blushed. "A date. I'll go out with you. Or in—I mean we can stay in. Or whatever. But yes, Charlie. I'm in."

"Ace," he said again and then told me he'd call in the morning and hung up. It was late.

He sure had the knack for leaving a girl wanting more.

*

Tuesday I ate enough Life Savers to sink a ship. I had stopped smoking eight years before and hadn't felt the craving for something like a smoke for a very long time. But I had it now. Because my brain was a hamster on a wheel. Now that

I'd agreed to see him, for real, I couldn't shake the image of him from my mind. Or the remembrance of the way his hands felt on me. Or those kisses—Jesus, those kisses. So much more addictive than anything I'd ever encountered. If I shut my eyes it was easy to call up the scent of him, the feel of him, and the sound of his voice. It was all so damn easy that I could barely focus on my work.

Hence the LifeSavers. Every time I felt too spacey, too electric, every time that I hit a point where in the past I'd have gone out and smoked, I popped a candy. By the time lunchtime hit, the assistant office manager Sue asked me if I was trying to destroy my teeth in a single day.

"Every time you crunch down on one of those things I cringe," she laughed. "I imagine it's your teeth fracturing, not that candy."

I gasped. "Gee, thanks for that image, Sue!" I laughed and swallowed my crushed candy currently coating my tongue. "But now I'll stop chewing them because I'm paranoid."

She shrugged. "Maybe it's me. I cracked a tooth on a Gobstopper in college and never looked back. I don't chew hard stuff and apparently it freaks me out when others do," she laughed.

"Coffee," I said.

She raised an eyebrow at me. "I'm not sure coffee is what you need. A nice cup of chamomile maybe."

"I'm not a hundred," I snorted.

"Or a nice sedative," she teased.

"Is it that obvious?" I asked, softly, leaning close as we stood at the copy counter. Her making stacks of outgoing mail, me rifling stacks of stuff that had come from my inbox.

"That you're all hopped up over something? Yes!"

"Ugh." I hung my head. "Pathetic."

He texted me at five. I was pulling out of the parking lot, feeling as if I'd swallowed a live wire. I glanced at the text before pulling into traffic.

SOON, ACE, SOON ☺

I couldn't help but laugh. It was the innocent looking smiley face that looked out of place with what felt like a sensually malicious message. Soon, I'll get my hands on you. Soon, I'll press my body to yours. Soon, I'll kiss you, touch you, enter you until you…

I jumped when the person behind me honked and then I shot through the green light ahead of me. Good thing I didn't work far from home or I'd probably get in an accident before I got there. I'd told him I'd go home and change and then call him.

It was snowing again.

I took my work clothes off and felt like I was shedding a too small skin for one that could breathe. I found a pale pink camisole, so pale it was practically nude, and slid it on over my black bra. Then a cream colored, deep V neck sweater that was warm but not too bulky.

"I want to look like a woman, not a linebacker," I whispered. I settled on dark wash straight leg jeans, my favorite brown leather boots and minimal makeup. My red lipstick from work replaced by a softer rose. I brushed my teeth three times until I feared for the enamel. Then I stood staring at my cell phone on the foyer table like it might rear up and bite me.

It buzzed and I yelped. Then I read the message with shaking fingers. I'd pick him up in ten minutes.

That way I was in control. I didn't have to worry that I was at someone's mercy. I didn't have to obsess over lack of control. My kids would be the first to tell you I'm a control freak. Scratch that, my ex would probably be the first. But I was a single woman going out with a new guy and no matter how angelic he looked…

"You can never be too careful," I told myself.

I grabbed my phone, wrote his name, address and number on an index card and left it dead center on my desk blotter. That way if I disappeared, Louise and the kids would have information about the number one suspect. I filled Elliot's food bowl and walked out. I left the front porch light and the foyer lamp on. I was all out of excuses. Time to go.

Sommer Marsden

CHAPTER FIVE

"I can't be out late," I said by way of hello when Charlie opened the door. "I have to get up at 5:30," I barreled on.

He laughed and I was caught off guard again by the way his eyes crinkled when he was amused. It aged him just a touch and gave him an air of wisdom unusual for someone his age.

"Coming to the door ready with the excuses," he teased.

I hung my head and toed the brick work of his front steps with my boot. "Yeah. That was shitty, wasn't it?"

"You want to come in or you want me to come out?" he asked.

I bit my lip, considered it. I was having trouble focusing on anything beyond my wildly beating heart. My first date since divorcing Jack and the guy was seventeen years younger than me.

"I'll come in for a moment. While we figure…" I shrugged. "While we talk."

His foyer was small. More of a very short narrow hall that I could see opened into a larger room. Probably the living room. But he leaned against the wall, smiling a small half smile that seemed to burrow hotly into the very center of me.

"What did you want to do? Whatever you want, Ace. We can stay in. We can go out. We can stand here in the hall and chat." He laughed softly, tilted his head back against the pale blue wall and watched me. His eyes in this light, at that angle were damn near feline. He was patient too because he simply stood there waiting for me to think.

I wiggled my toes inside my boots, clamped my thighs together, and realized that created a quite sexual sensation that made it even more difficult to breathe at the moment. "Um…where would we go if we went out?"

"Where do you want to go?"

I rolled my eyes and sighed. "Help me out here, Charlie. I feel like I'm going to climb out of my skin. You, however, seem very calm."

"We could go to this club up the street."

I chewed my lip. "Not much of a clubber."

He chuckled. "There's a nice quiet bar up the road that serves Tapas as well as craft beers."

I didn't say anything.

"Or we can stay here. I can ply you with liquor, stain your virtue."

It was my turn to laugh. But it was loud and nervous in the tight space.

He reached out and simply took my hand. His thumb ran up and back along my skin. "I could make you some food. I could try and keep you from flying off into space."

Another strangled laugh from me and then I looked him in the eye. His eyes were sincere and dark blue this close. When he leaned in and kiss me I didn't fight it. If anything, I welcomed it, sighing so deeply it seemed to come from my toes. My mind shot back to the night before. That first kiss.

I kissed him back, touched his cheeks and said, "Thank you, Charlie."

He pulled back to look at me and said, "For what?"

"For that first kiss last night."

He took a step toward me and brought us closer together in the dim foyer. Harsh yellow light came in through the upper pane of glass in the front door. The light sliced across the side of his face giving him a semi-angelic glow. The heat coming off him was overtaking me. I panted a little, part warmth, part excitement.

"Why are you thanking me?" His hands skimmed up my sides inside my open coat, barely petting my sweater but doing it hard enough that I was supremely aware of being touched. More so than if he'd done it with a heavier hand.

"Because it's been twenty years since I had a first kiss from a man. Twenty years since I've had a first anything with a man. And…"

His fingers stroked my hair and he kissed my forehead. I found it both endearing and sexy, that chaste little kiss. "And it was okay."

I found my bravery, took his face in my hands, feeling the bite of stubble on my palms. I kissed him roughly, and then delivered a few delicious little flicks with my tongue. "It was far from okay," I murmured. "It was amazing."

He growled playfully from my boldness and then stepped forward again, closing the final space between us. "In or out, Ace? What are we doing? Because if we just stand here, smashed together in this narrow little room, I'm going to have to take your clothes off."

I gasped but excitement flared through me. "In," I said. "Can you cook? Because if you can't, I can."

"Oh, I can cook," he said. "Among other things." He took my hand and led me further into his apartment.

*

He wasn't kidding. I sat at the breakfast island in his small kitchen. I was perched on a tall-backed barstool with a plaid cushion. Content to watch him work. He chopped up potatoes and onions for a frittata. I sipped from a glass of Merlot and marveled at the way he moved around the kitchen.

"I could have made you something better but I didn't get to shop today."

"Cheese and onion and potato and egg and ham," I said. "What's wrong with that? Nothing could *be* better."

He glanced up at me, but instead of the grin I anticipated, he simply remained slightly serious and watched me. "Are you still nervous?" he asked.

"Intensely," I said.

He frowned slightly.

"You have to understand, I was with one man for almost twenty years."

"That's a long time."

"Especially when you actually remain monogamous," I laughed. Then I chewed my lip wishing I could suck the words back in. Not the discussion I wanted to have on a first date.

I inspected my brightly colored wine glass. It was rainbow striped and when I looked at his apartment through the bands of color it turned everything into a Christmas card.

"I won't ask," he said, softly cranking the heat beneath a cast iron skillet. "But his loss is something, I will say."

I shrugged. "We grew apart," I said. "I changed. He didn't. It was that simple. But we have two amazing kids," I said. "Twins."

"Still can't believe you're a mother," he said, shaking his head. There was that grin I'd anticipated and it went straight to the core of me.

"What are your plans, Charlie?" Then I swallowed hard because it dawned on me, maybe he didn't have any. Maybe he was simply working menial jobs to live the way he wanted and travel when he wanted and be as he wanted. I'd just read a book like that. The guy worked wherever he could find work so he could have less but live more.

"My plans are to have fun while I figure out my plans," he said. "I went to school. Got my AA. Figured by the time I got out I'd know what I wanted to do with myself. And yet..." He gave the potatoes and onion a stir and then turned the flame down. "As you can see, I am still working at the pharmacy. I haven't decided."

I nodded. "But that's okay." It's what I'd told my kids. Some people had a harder time figuring themselves out. Some people never did. But you should live a damn fine life anyway.

"It is. I am studying this, studying that, and waiting for the lightning bolt. I'm poor though, seeing as I haven't become a fantastic surgeon or a brilliant writer. So I take these classes online from this amazing place. They offer classes from large universities for free."

The more he talked, the more I wanted to kiss him. Put my fingers in that dark curly hair and hold him to me and kiss him. He had more scruff today. Almost a beard but not quite. And even though I normally hated facial hair, on him it worked. Hugely.

"That is amazing. Do you get credit?"

He topped off my wine. "Nope. But some Profs will send you a certificate of completion. I figure when I find one that really does it for me, I'll scrounge the money to take some courses at Towson. Until then, I'm working and dabbling."

"Working and dabbling," I said softly. "That sounds amazing…"

And it did. It sounded brave and exciting and like sheer perfection.

He traced my index finger with his. It was like being struck by that lightning bolt he spoke of. "You should try some. They're free after all. Take a nutrition course, learn about nuclear medicine, and appreciate the shit out of some art."

I snickered. Charlie slid the pan into the oven and came behind the island. He planted a hand on either side of my seat and kissed me.

"I'm appreciating the shit out of you," I mumbled, laughing at myself.

He slid his fingers along my neck, cupped the back of my head, anchored me so he could deepen the kiss. His checkered shirt was soft against my skin, his beard scratchy against my cheek. The kiss was the kind that curls your toes. The kind of kiss I'd forgotten, for a very long time, existed.

"I'm appreciating you, too, Ace." Charlie placed open mouthed kisses down along my neck, pulling my sweater to the side to put a few along my shoulder. I shivered from the soft warmth of his mouth. He moved my camisole strap and then my bra strap and licked the skin where they'd been.

My nipples pebbled hard and a hot, a steady pulse started between my legs. I had a very vivid flash of him naked, burying his cock in me. My pussy clenched tight and eager around nothing at the mental image. I groaned softly.

He laughed. ""Yeah?" he said to my groan.

"Yeah," I sighed. "Charlie, I have to say...no sex. No sex. I'm not ready. I mean, fuck..." I pulled back to look into those bright alert eyes. "I am ready. My body is ready like you wouldn't believe. But..." I took his hand and put it above my pounding heart. If he was as good a guy as he seemed, if he was as amazing as I thought he was, he'd understand. "In here I'm not quite ready yet. I'm scared, if you want me to be honest."

"I get it," he said against my throat. He kissed my cheek, my forehead, my eyelids. I shivered again at that. It was a fairly innocent gesture so why did I find it so amazingly sexy?

"Take a shower with me," he said.

A shocked burble of laughter came out of me and I put my hands on his chest, pushing him back a step. "Didn't you hear me?"

"I did." He grinned at me. Didn't try to touch me. He simply stood there with my hands splayed against his blue checkered shirt.

"I just said—"

"No sex," he said.

"Yes, no sex."

"I don't want to have sex."

"But a shower—"

He cut me off again. "It's water. It's bathing. It's me and you in an intimate setting, naked, touching, but no sex." He put his hands up and plastered his most innocent look on his face. "No. Sex." He repeated.

The oven timer went off and his eyes wandered to the frittata.

"Charlie—"

"Hold that thought," he said.

He went over, checked our dinner and brought it out to cool. "It only needs a few minutes," he muttered. "Just to set."

"Now about that shower," I said, my voice a tad too strangled for my taste.

He held his hand out. "Yes, Abby. About that shower. Come with me."

"I didn't say yes," I whispered.

"You didn't say no," he said, touching my hand but only briefly.

"Why?" I asked. Because I simply had to know.

He shrugged, coming around to stand in front of me again. His jeans were low on his hips. Not too tight, not too loose. And God, how I wanted to see them off him. "Because I want to see you. I want to touch you. Smell you. Kiss you..."

He was mesmerizing. I felt hypnotized. The snake to his charmer. The nail to his magnet. The dog to his whistle. The last fleeting thought made me laugh.

"That's funny?" he asked, cocking his head. But he seemed amused, not offended.

"No." I shook my head. "My own panicked thoughts are amusing."

"Come on. I swear to you. No sex. Think of it as an appetizer. In fact," he wound his fingers through mine and heat seared along my skin. It was like being burned in the most luscious and sensual way. "I promise you that if—no, *when*—you want that sex you're so dead set against, I won't let you. I will, in fact, turn you down."

Now I was laughing in earnest. "Oh, yeah?"

He turned my hand in his and kissed the underside of my wrist. The skin there was fragile and sensitive and the pressure of his lips was nearly overwhelming. Just talking to him, watching his body language and hearing his voice, had me panting slightly. Wanting a kiss. Wanting him to touch me. Christ, wanting so much more and then some.

But, yes, I was scared. Rose had called me an accidental cougar, I felt, at the moment, more like an accidental virgin. It was as if I couldn't remember what to do, how to be, in this situation. So I simply took a breath and let him guide me.

"Okay, fine," I said, despite my nagging worry. "I'll shower with you. But the sex...I won't want it."

Even as I said it, I felt like a liar.

He chuckled. "Okay, Ace, whatever you say."

Then he tugged my arm lightly and I stood. He wrapped his arms around me, kissed me for real. So thoroughly I felt it in my gut. Then he pressed his mouth to my ear and said, "Right this way. One shower, coming up."

I shook my head as I followed him. What was I thinking? I must have lost my damn mind.

CHAPTER SIX

When he undressed me, I held my breath. Put my hands up like a child in order to let him pull off my sweater and then my camisole. Charlie took a moment to study me and I kept my big fat mouth shut. Refused to give into the urge to make excuses for my forty-two year old semi-nudity.

I was what I was and that happened to be the person he'd flirted with. Smiled at. Asked out. But part of me, the part that had been alone for a while, wondered if now, looking at me in a bra and jeans, he felt cheated. If I was less than he'd bargained for.

He used his fingertip to trace the lace along my bra cup. Then he brushed my nipple through the sheer fabric until it stood up tight and sensitive.

"I have a feeling," he said softly, "that if I told you how beautiful you are you'd blow it off. Or laugh." Before I could speak he leaned forward, tugged my bra cup down and sucked my bare nipple into his mouth.

The pressure coursed through me from breast to pussy and stole my breath. Any words I would have used to disregard his compliment were lost in the ether.

"But you are," he went on, giving my left nipple the same sweet attention so that my body arched forward toward his of its own accord. "Beautiful," he said. Then he took my bra off and dropped it on top of my sweater.

My jeans succumbed to his fingers next and then my panties. By the time I was bare I could hardly breathe. "You need to take your clothes off fast," I said.

My tongue didn't want to work. It felt twice as big as it should and unwieldy.

Charlie laughed softly, pulling off his socks and unbuckling he belt. "Why is that?"

"Because I feel very alone all naked and exposed." I put my hand out, even though it felt somewhat disembodied, and popped the button on his jeans. My fingers were stiff and clueless but I soldiered on and pulled down his zipper.

Every inch of him that became exposed increased my heart rate. I feared death by nudity in a twenty-something's bathroom while a wonderful, fragrant frittata cooled to an inedible temperature on the counter.

I snorted and he caught my wrist. "Share the joke."

"I'm wondering if I might die naked in your bathroom is all. My poor kids. What would they write in the obituary?"

He pushed me against the wall, his jeans and his boxers down around his hips but still on. "Don't worry. You won't die, Ace. But you will come. I promise you that."

"I thought—"

"No sex," he said. "Don't worry. But Abby…" He kissed my clavicle and then licked a hot line from my neck to my breasts to my belly button. "You're a smart woman, you know there are multiple ways to have an orgasm that do not include sex."

"Oh," I said on a puff of air. It was the only thing I could think to say.

I pushed his jeans down, felt the heat and smoothness of his skin. He shucked them by shimmying his hips as he pulled his checkered shirt open. The tiny snaps made little metallic popping sounds as he pulled.

His chest was smooth and hard and rippled. So rippled that I had to touch him to make sure he was real. He looked like something out of a clothing ad and I had that moment of panic again. What was I doing here? What was I thinking? But then I shut that chattering, clamoring part of my mind down and observed. I noticed how Charlie was looking at me and my worries fell away.

He looked pleased. Happy. Turned on. I had nothing to worry about so it was time to stop acting like a fool and enjoy this new experience. This excitement and acceptance and arousal.

I touched him and his big blue eyes drifted shut. His cock was more than I'd even anticipated. Heavy and long in my hand, responding brilliantly to every small squeeze I delivered. I found my bravery, and leaned forward to brush soft kisses along the slope of his throat. I ran my tongue across his Adam's apple and then delivered a small, soft bite to his collar bone.

"Ace," he chuckled, eyes still shut. Then they popped open even as I began to stroke him softly. I found that once I was touching him I simply wanted to touch him more. "Does that bother you?" he asked.

"What?" I squeezed and those amazing eyes drifted shut again. But just for a second.

"Ace?"

I shook my head. "I've grown rather attached to it, actually."

"Good." He moved away from me and I felt the absence of him. So much so that it startled me.

Charlie pushed back the curtain, turned on the water and then shook his head. "I'm a lobster red kind of guy. I take showers so hot I glow. Lucky for me the guy who owns this monstrosity of a house put a new, supersized hot water heater in before I rented."

"I thought you were green," I teased.

"My penance is walking to work."

"Ah, smart. Get away with one by doing the other."

He pointed at me and my chest great hot. I knew without even looking in his small ancient medicine cabinet mirror that it was red with lust.

"Now you're catching on."

"Well, it's your lucky day," I said. "I also am a lobster red showerer…er."

"Ah," he said, letting his head tilt back. My eyes drifted to his cock. Hard and northward pointing as he stood there bent over feeling the water. "I knew I chose the right woman."

My insides flustered at his words. It felt like a flock of tiny birds in my stomach had all preened at once. I stepped toward Charlie when he held his hand out and together we stepped in. "This is kind of a torturous thing isn't it?" I asked. "If we're not going to…have sex."

"Torturous, maybe. But sweet," he said.

Beneath the torrent of hot water he kissed me again and I willingly opened my mouth and submitted to that kiss. Feeling my heartbeat in my clitoris when he pressed himself close to me and his erection nestled perfectly against my nether lips.

I was reconsidering that no sex thing.

He unhooked the shower head and pushed the notch so it became a hard, concentrated stream. Then he handed it to me. My fingers curled around the wand before he even spoke. "Now I want to see you," he said, smiling slightly. It was a devilish smile. Mischievous.

"See me what?"

"See you get off," he said. "If I can't have you, I want to see you. Show me."

*

"I can't," I whispered. Certain there was no way he could hear me above the rush of the water.

"You can," he said. Then he took my hand and angled that stream, aiming. The hard stream hit my pussy and somehow the strength of it kissed my clit briefly. I jumped, gasping. What would that feel like if I did it myself? If I truly focused that hard rush of water on that tender organ?

He groaned. "See, just that little reaction could make me come."

I shut my eyes. "You're filthy," I said. But I could feel a smile spread across my face.

He angled the stream again and again the water pounded against my hard clit. "But you love it," he said.

I did as he asked. I stood and I parted my legs. With shaking fingers I spread my pussy lips back and aimed the hard, hot spray at my clit. Charlie sank down to sit on the edge of the tub after pushing the shower curtain out. We'd flood his floor but he didn't seem to care about that.

I shut my eyes, tilted my head back, and tried to soak in the feeling of the moment. Magical, secretive, silent. He was watching. I was performing. Nothing but the whoosh of water and a big exciting scary thrill of something new. *Someone* new.

I made a soft noise as everything seemed to grow more sensitive. My pussy grew tighter, I could feel everything plumping up, readying for release. I wanted to go back on my words from earlier and grab him, pull him to me, beg him to take me. It had been way too long for me. But it had been even longer since I'd felt the buzz and intoxication of a new lover.

Instead, I focused on the mental image of him touching me. The remembered feel of his kisses. Lost in that, growing closer, I jumped when he wrapped his hands around the neck of the shower head and said, "May I?"

"I—" The words died on my lips and I simply nodded, releasing my grip on the showerhead. He brushed my wet hand aside and spread my pussy lips himself. Just the visual of him touching me there made my knees dip. The feel of his fingers pressed to that sensitive skin caused a small bout of lightheadedness.

"I want it right there," he said. "Right where it's the rosiest." His mouth was a tight line of concentration and I found it so endearing. I reached out, touched his wet hair. But then the water hit its mark, my belly muscles contracted and pleasure bled through me at an alarming rate.

"Oh…" I said. And then I sighed, thinking of nothing beyond the obvious to say.

"Right here," he said. But he moved the spray away, bathing my outer lips with it, the tops of my thighs, my belly.

"Charlie," I said without thinking.

He chuckled, dipped his head and bit his tongue. Then he put me out of my misery and directed the stream back where I needed it. I came, my fingers curled in his wet wavy hair, the sound of his happy laughter in my ears.

Before I could open my eyes, Charlie was standing, pressing against me—kissing me. I grasped his cock, pulled him even closer to deliver my own hungry kiss. His mouth was soft and sweet and his tongue swept over mine with a passion I couldn't remember feeling.

"I changed my mind about that sex," I whispered, raising one leg to hook it against his trim waist. Opening my body to him so he could feel how hot and wet I was. Wet enough to rival the shower.

He looked down at me, licking his lips as if tasting my kiss. "I haven't," he said. "I told you I wouldn't let you, and I meant it."

"But—"

"I will feed you reheated frittata, though," he said.

"At least let me see you," I said in my best coaxing tone.

"Later," he said. One more kiss and he was cutting the water, taking my hand, leading me out to dry me with a huge green towel.

"But—" I said again, slightly sex-stunned. He was still nude and my God, spectacular.

"I'm a man of my word," he said. His eyes were the same color as new denim, seemingly darker with arousal. "But I'll feed you, pretty lady."

"Yes," I said. "Feed me. Something. Because I'm having a little sexual frustration here," I whispered.

He took my hand, squeezed and whispered, "Patience, Ace."

*

I took the final bite of my frittata. Since my hands had stopped shaking, I was able to focus. The rush of the orgasm, the rush of him watching me and then taking over, had shaken me more than I thought it would.

He was watching me and smiling. "Good?"

"Excellent. You're very talented. Did you take cooking classes? Is that one of your things you've tried?" He poured me more wine.

"Yeah, I took a short course. But I liked to cook before that. I just took the course to learn things like soufflés and how to poach eggs and stuff." He shrugged. "It was fun."

I must have been in the mood to ask questions because I heard myself ask, "Why did you give me a second look Friday?"

Charlie looked genuinely surprised. "Why wouldn't I?"

It was my turn to shrug. "Why would you? I'm a bit older than you."

"Man, you really care about those numbers, don't you?" he said, frowning slightly. He took my plate after I waved off his offer of another slice. "I saw a beautiful woman," he said, placing our plates in the sink. "I looked twice. I would have looked twice at you Abby if you'd been twenty or thirty or sixty. You were beautiful to me, all windblown and red cheeked. Sitting in that bright winter sun."

I looked down, fiddled with my napkin.

"Look at me please."

I did. Trying to train my focus on his kind eyes and not do that cheating thing where you look at the bridge of someone's nose.

"I think you're beautiful. Will you ever be able to accept that for what it is without slapping a label on it?"

"Yes…" I stammered. "I think so."

"Good."

He pulled me to standing and led me into the living room.

The room was small but cozy with an off white sofa and an old fireplace that no longer functioned from the looks of it. What made me laugh was he'd put a small ceramic heater inside the fireplace set on low. It glowed electric red and orange.

"Very clever," I said.

We sat and he put his arm around me. "I am a very clever boy," he whispered, "even if I do say so myself."

We sat and sipped wine. I heard the wind outside and realized that I wasn't in any hurry to step out of his warm apartment or his warm arms and go out into that late winter cold. But it was getting late…

"I can tell you're thinking about leaving," he whispered.

We didn't have the TV on. We didn't have music on. It was just me and Charlie sitting in silence watching the fiery glow of a heater tucked into a fireplace.

And I found that it was perfect.

I let my head fall back and whispered back. "How can you tell? Are you psychic, Charlie?"

"No. But I can read you for some reason. Another perk." He slid his hand along the nape of my neck and pulled me in for a kiss. A long kiss. An in-depth kiss. My body warmed and felt as if it was blossoming for him. I found myself regretting my no sex proclamation and yet not. The messing around, the extended foreplay, the teasing…it was all so delicious and wonderful.

So much more than I'd ever anticipated with him. *He* was so much more than I'd ever anticipated.

Charlie sucked my tongue gently, let his big hands smooth along my shoulders, my arm, my collar bone. He touched my thigh, my hip, my waist. But he never strayed where I wanted him most. And he did it on purpose. I knew when I was being toyed with. I knew when I was being tantalized.

I broke free of the kiss and looked at him. He looked as stunned and shiny-eyed as I felt. I smiled, touched his lower lip. His tongue darted out to touch my skin.

"I want to see you," I said. "I really do. You saw me, Charlie. Tit for tat."

His eyes dropped obviously to my chest and he grinned. "Ace, did you have to say tit?"

I chuckled. Then I found my boldness nestled deep inside me and woke it up. I pulled at his belt, his jeans. "Show me."

He sighed. "That might kill me."

"Might," I said. "And you know what they say. What doesn't kill you makes you stronger."

"I don't know if that's uplifting or not," he laughed.

But then his cock was out and in his hand. He'd yanked his shirt up to his chest. Charlie was hard. Hard enough to send a wet tremble through the very center of me. God, how I wanted him. Why was I waiting?

Because I was, that was why. It was as simple as that.

I put his hand on his erection and sat back, smiling. "Now you."

It was closing in on midnight. Somehow the time between me arriving and the witching hour had flown. It had gone in a blink and I marveled at it.

He dragged his fist up his length, squeezed. His broad thumb brushed over the top of his cock, spreading a shiny bit of pre-come on the tip. I heard myself sigh. Saw him smile.

"You know…" I said softly.

"Nope. No sex. I promised you." He leaned over and kissed me again, His mouth pressing sweetly to mine and then my jaw, my neck. All the while I could feel him jacking his cock, the movements getting rougher.

The thrill that coursed through me was humbling. I felt

all-powerful. Sensual. Amazing. The more he kissed me, the more aggressively he handled himself. I kept my eyes open. Watching him, taking it all in.

"You smell so good," he laughed.

"I smell like you," I countered. "Your shower. My hair is still wet for god's sake!"

He chuckled, pushed me back with tented fingers and we both watched as he stroked himself. His trim hips shot up and I marveled at the way they flexed. The set of his jaw, his breathing, the tension in his taut chest, the flex in his belly muscles—it all belied pleasure about to come to a peak.

Then he opened his hand, yanked up his jeans and pulled me to him, kissing me. "Not tonight," he said.

A small clock on the mantle began to tick off the hour. Midnight.

"Are you turning into a pumpkin?" I groaned.

I felt him smile against my cheek even as he delivered another kiss to the side of my face. 'Nope. The first time I come with you…I want to come with you. But I am going to tell you, next time. Next time you can watch me come. Next time you can help me…"

He let the words hang there and I found myself struggling for air. "Okay," I said. "Okay. I have to go."

I felt tipsy with lust. Heavy headed. Wild inside. I stood and he hugged me tight. The hug was as good as the kiss, I thought. And then somehow in a blur, he was shutting my car door with me inside and I was driving off.

At my house, Elliot waited with accusing eyes. I gave him more kibble and stuck my tongue out at him. Louise was also waiting in the form of a message in my phone to call her immediately when I got home. No matter how late.

I obliged.

"Did you kiss him?"

"Yes."

"Did you go out?"

"No. We stayed in."

"Did you sleep with him, you dirty girl?"

"Nope," I said, smiling. Because I was telling the truth. I fell asleep remembering him watching me. Those blue eyes studying me as if I were a work of art. The feel of his silken skin in my hand, long and hard. The sound he made when he was close. And the kiss he gave me when he bundled me off into the dark, cold night. Without letting me see him come.

I'd gotten no tit for my tat. But I couldn't hold that against Charlie. The only thing I wanted to hold against Charlie was myself.

CHAPTER SEVEN

"How's that zinc working out?" Cathleen asked Wednesday morning.

I couldn't help but smile. A ridiculously big smile for such a simple question. "Well," I said. "It made me feel a lot better."

When I said it, in my mind, I was reliving the shower scene between us. Him holding that showerhead, angling it my way, intuiting everything I needed to get me off without ever touching me.

She frowned. "Are you sure? You still look a little flushed. You might want to try some more. Or go home, have a hot toddy and go right to bed."

I swallowed a burble of laughter. I was flushed because I was experiencing filthy memories, but she was so sweet and so concerned I couldn't laugh. "I'll consider that," I said.

"In fact, I'm going to make a nice cup of chai tea, want one? With organic vanilla syrup? Might help the tickle."

I cleared my throat again. "Sure. I'd love that, actually."

She smiled, happy to be helping, and scurried off in her plaid skirt, black flats and cream colored sweater. She reminded me of the virgin sorority girl. All goodness and light and helpfulness.

My phone went off and I reached in my jacket pocket expecting, as usual, Louise or Rose or even occasionally Heath. Instead it said Charlie and he'd kept it succinct:

I CAN'T STOP THINKING ABOUT YOU. ABOUT ME AND YOU. ABOUT YOU UNDER ME.

I smiled and texted him back:

JUST DISCUSSING ZINC HERE.

The phone vibrated.

ARE YOU SICK FOR REAL?

I laughed softly. My fingers felt a little vibratey themselves as I spelled out:

I'VE BEEN ADVISED TO GO HOME AND GO RIGHT TO BED AFTER WORK.

Then:

HOPE YOU FEEL BETTER.

I answered:

I'M SURE I WILL…

I paused, fingers shaking outright now. My stomach felt like I was in free fall. I whispered, "Fuck it" and finished the text:

WANT TO COME HAVE HOT TODDIES IN BED WITH ME?

There was a long pause. Longer than any other. Longer than I liked. When the phone vibrated in response I almost dropped it.

IS THAT EVEN A REAL QUESTION? WHAT TIME?

I didn't allow myself to think. I answered:

SIX. SEE YOU THERE.

When the phone shivered in my hand again, a burble of laughter slipped out of me.

I'LL BE THERE. WITH BELLS ON. DING-DONG ☺

I couldn't help but laugh and then I was being handed a cup of hot chai tea. "Here you are, this will help you feel better," Cathleen said.

I sipped it. "Thanks, Cat. I feel better already."

*

I took off work an hour early and got home about quarter after four. "You're doing this," I told myself. My stomach was abuzz with nerves but I cherished it. I hadn't felt this alive, this amazing, in a very long time. Every breath was a gift, every hear beat a jolt of vibrancy.

I fed Elliot and then coached him that Charlie was coming over and to behave himself and above all else, "No claws," I warned.

He looked at me like I was speaking Chinese and then proceeded to eat his kibble with a bored expression.

Steam filled the bathroom and I added a lavender tablet to the bottom of the shower. I then proceeded to wash my hair, exfoliate my skin and shave…everything. Not for Charlie. He hadn't seemed to care one way or the other the night before. I had turned him on 'as is' but I wanted to feel smooth and pretty and put together.

When it came to pubic hair I started to shave, but then hesitated. I wasn't one for the completely bare look—or as I often viewed it, the prepubescent look. So I compromised by shaving the sides and then neatly clipping the rest. My hands shook as I did it because it occurred to me that I was primping myself for sex. I was readying myself to be with him.

"Don't stab yourself in the hoo-ha with clipping scissors," I whispered. Elliot chose that moment to stick his calico head into the bathroom. It gave me the giggles so I sat there, naked, legs spread, on the edge of the tub laughing. The very picture of insanity.

When I finally got myself under control, I rinsed off, brushed my teeth, reapplied makeup and took a deep breath.

Staring back at me from the mirror was still a forty-two year old woman. With bright blue eyes that had a fairy ring of green around the pupil. She still had very fine lines beginning at the edges of her eyes that were more pronounced when she smiled. She still had the bizarre mix of very high sharp cheekbones and a round face. She still had lips a bit too thin for my taste and a bottom tooth that was crooked to the point of annoyance. She still looked nervous.

"But pretty," I told the woman in the mirror. Then I pointed at her. "And determined. Because have you *seen* Charlie? He's beyond handsome. If he just wanted to get laid he could go do that in a heartbeat. There's something about you," I said. Then changed it. "There's something about *me* that attracts him."

I sighed, feeling the nerves welling up inside me. Then I shut my eyes and breathed some more. Deep yoga breaths that calmed my kicking heart. "It's okay," I said. And then: "But now you have to stop talking to yourself because it's creepy."

I stopped talking to myself. Instead, I found my old red and white cookbook and looked up hot toddies. I was serious. We were going to get in my bed with hot toddies and drink them. Just like Benjamin Franklin or John Hancock or whoever the fuck it was I'd read about drinking them when I was younger.

"Details are not important," I said to myself. Then Elliot rubbed my ankle and I shrieked and jumped. "Jesus Christ, Abby, nervous much?" I whispered.

I got out my whiskey and spices.

I was measuring out the spices when it hit me. "Shit, I might want to feed him first or we could end up in bed, too drunk to do it."

That seemed impossible but I couldn't take the chance. I phoned the takeout place on the corner and they arrived twenty minutes later with an array of junk I'd never normally eat but seemed like a good idea when I was standing at the phone nervous and hungry.

Mozzarella sticks, chicken wings, fried zucchini, potato skins and just to save my soul, a big chef salad.

"There." The doorbell rang again and I scurried to it, thinking the delivery man had forgotten to give me something. When I opened it, instead of a short young man in a Danny's pizza shirt, I found Charlie. Tall, dark, handsome Charlie. In an open bomber jacket wearing a blue flannel shirt that begged to be stroked and enough scruff on his face to make me weak in the knees.

"You're early," I blurted.

He stepped inside and I found myself backing up a step, heart thundering.

"I'm sorry. Do you want me to go?"

"N-n-no." The word finally came out. I watched him. His eyes were dark and brooding. His mouth was set. He wasn't smiling. I blundered on. "I'm not done making the drinks," I said. "And there's foo—"

He cut the word off by grabbing my upper arms and pulling me toward him. His mouth pressed roughly to mine and it was part gasp, part desire that caused me to open my lips so fast. His tongue was sweet as if he'd been eating candy and I felt a rush of heat and moisture between my legs.

"I'm sorry, you can shut me down if you want, but I don't

want that drink yet. And I don't want the food. I want you. And I waited as long as I could."

I blinked. He was holding my shoulders, looking me in the eye, baring his soul and god, it was so weird but he seemed so serious. So fucking serious I felt a little humbled and a lot staggered by it. "I...um..."

He kissed me again and buried his hands in my hair. Charlie pressed his body against mine and I felt every hard plane and angle. I felt the exquisite press of his cock to the split of my pussy and I made a fleeting bizarre wish for my pants to evaporate right then and there.

"Don't be mad," he said.

Just as he said it, I embraced the whole crazy thing. I slipped my hands down his trim hips, cradled them as I kissed him back. And then I found him with my hand, stroking him through his dark jeans. He arched his hips and hissed like he'd been burned.

He paused, sighing, and said, "But wait. You're not sick, are you? I'm not being an asshole, am I?"

I laughed as I ran a single fingertip along the ridge of his erection. "Nope. Not sick. I was flushed, my cheeks were red and a girl at work assumed I was sick but I was..." I pulled the top button of his button fly.

"You were...?" he groaned, watching me.

"But I was flushed because I was thinking about you." I tugged and the second button released.

"Me?" He chewed his lower lip. I recognized the gesture because I did it. It was sexy and endearing and made me feel suddenly like the hunter, not the hunted.

"Yes, you. You were in my head. Last night. What we did. What you *didn't* do and I was just...a little warm," I laughed.

Tug. The third button released.

He grabbed my wrists, his grip tight, and desire ignited white-hot in my stomach and much-much lower.

"You're going to have to forgive me," he said and then walked me to the wall and pushed me to it. Charlie had lost his patient, Mr.-Nice-Guy way of thinking. The kiss he delivered was the most hungry I could remember. The feel of his lips and tongue and teeth clashing with mine, thrilling.

He pushed my black sweater up, found me bare underneath and made a noise that was more animal than man. My mind tried to panic. Tried to inform me that I was senior to him, had had two children, all the things we worry have destroyed us for men. But that noise—oh, that noise—wiped every stray and troublesome thought away. And if any had lingered, the feel of his warm, soft lips closing over my nipple, followed swiftly by a hot swipe of his wet tongue shut the remaining ones down in a heartbeat.

He pushed his fingers beneath the waistband of my gray leggings and my skin seemed to hum. My brain buzzed in unison. I was as high as I'd ever been but so stone cold sober I absorbed every nuance of the passing seconds.

"Take them off," he said, fingers sweeping lower to find that beneath the leggings I was bare of undergarments as well. Another growl and before my adrenaline-charged hands could do his bidding, he pushed them down roughly to my knees and grabbed my hips. "Better yet, I'll do it."

"You don't want your toddy?" I asked, stupidly.

There was a pregnant pause. A moment that stretched a year. And then he smiled and my pussy flexed wetly at nothing more than the devilish curve of his lips. "No. I'll pass. We can have it after."

I nodded, breathless.

"Bedroom or right damn here, Ace? Because you're

running out of time. My patience has hit the non-existent range."

I pulled my legs free of my pants, left them puddled there by the wall and took his hand. "Come on."

"On…in…I plan to do all of them tonight."

My face and chest felt hot enough to burst into flames and I laughed a little high, a little wild, because I realized I hoped beyond hope that he meant exactly what he said.

"I had my tubes tied," I said bluntly as I pushed open my bedroom door. "And I'm clean. I just had an appointment with my—"

He pushed me back on the bed and his hands curled roughly in my sweater. I put my arms up instinctively as he tugged it over my head. Charlie smiled down at me. He was angelic, he was frightening, he was gorgeous. He was all of it rolled into one in the span of a single breath.

"I am also clean as a whistle. Believe it or not I have a printout in my wallet. I believe you. I want you. If you want a condom, though, I get it, I have those. I just want to stop talking and start fu—"

I grabbed his face, tugging his hair enough to make him grunt. I kissed him. "It's good, it's good," I said. I parted my legs and wrapped them around his waist, having a bizarre and sparkling moment of reality that this was actually happening. That I was actually there with him, naked, wet and ready. And eager, Christ, let's not forget eager.

Charlie raked his teeth along my neck. He bit gently on my clavicle and the pain it produced ran through me like a chill. He parted my nether lips with his fingers, stroking me tenderly so that in my mind I begged him to just touch me. For real. And he did. He pushed his thumb to my clit, rubbing just enough to make me grasp his shoulders and arch my hips. When he plunged a finger into me I exhaled as if relieved.

"You're very wet, Abby."

"You have no idea," I said, dumbly. I wasn't being very glib and I didn't care very much.

Charlie tsked at me, slipped another thick finger inside me and curled them together against my G-spot. "Oh, I think I do."

"Yes," I said. Just yes in general. Not yes to any particular thing other than the way he was making me feel.

He added a third finger and I gave him another yes. He smothered the tail end of my whispered word with another deep kiss. His mouth never stopped, trailing along my shoulder, my side, the very edges of my breasts. My nipples pebbled tightly and I curved up to meet his thrusting fingers. I felt on the verge of coming and it surprised the hell out of me. Jack had never, never, never been able to get me off with just his hands.

Charlie had no issues in that department. Whether it was the newness of this thing or the way he touched me or just how fucking long it had been since I'd gotten laid, with one more thrust and curl of his fingers, I came. Shivering forcefully with the release as if I had a fever. My breath caught and then I was laughing.

"Oh, I'm not done with you," he said, pulling at his jeans. Finishing the job I'd done of unbuttoning them. He shoved them down along with his navy blue briefs, my hands getting in the way and tangling him up until he finally chuckled, "Let me, Abby."

So I let him. Watching him unveil that flat belly, the slight rippling of his abs, the dark trail of hair from navel to cock. He was hard, gloriously hard and when he finally kicked his jeans to the floor and reared back on his knees to pull his shirt over his head, I sat up, took him in hand and then without thinking beyond wanting to feel that smooth warm skin against my lips, I took him into my mouth.

Charlie froze, his shirt still cowling his head. I couldn't see his face. All I could gauge was his body language and the change in his breathing. I slid my lips low, took him as far as I could and sucked.

"Jesus," he said. The first time I heard him sound anywhere near vulnerable. Anywhere near not one hundred percent self-assured.

I held his hips in my hands and dragged my tongue up and down his length, feeling all the ridges and dips of his skin. Then I sucked again, hard, and heard him inhale deeply. When I pulled back, not quite done, he decided I was. Charlie pushed me back and insinuated himself between my parted thighs.

"Enough of that," he said, voice raspy.

"What? You didn't like it?" I asked. I knew the answer, I was just teasing him. He knew it too because he hushed me, bumping my knees apart with his hips.

"Stop teasing me, Ace. I liked it too much. I could have let you keep going. I could have finished off that way."

He kissed me.

I licked his lower lip, kissed him with an urgency that had me flustered. "And you don't want to do that?"

"Hell no. I want to do this." His big hands slipped beneath my ass and he moved me up just an inch or two. The perfect amount for him to push into me slowly. It was maddening. With every inch of penetration his gaze grew more intense. He watched my face as he entered me and I wondered frantically if I looked as astonished as I felt.

It had been ages, I realized. Ages since I'd had sex. Ages

since someone had been inside my body, but even more ages since I had *felt* anything close to the sensation now pounding in the very center of my chest.

Freedom.

I gasped when he was fully seated in me. His pubic bone kissing my clitoris. My heartbeat pounding in my ears so loud it hushed the world.

His hands moved from my ass to my wrists. He pulled them above my head, held them there. "Okay?" he asked, not moving.

"Okay? Are you seriously asking me that?" I panted.

He laughed and the laugh took an amazing, handsome and kind man and made him even better. "I could probably come just from hearing you laugh," I said, watching his blue eyes study me.

"Yeah?"

"Yeah."

"Shall we test that theory?" he asked, rotating his hips just a touch.

"Hell no," I said.

And then Charlie started to move in earnest. Thrusting into me deep, holding my wrists just a shade too hard which made the whole fucking thing better. More intense. He dropped small kisses along my skin but sometimes the kisses turned to sharp, fast bites. Being off, not being able to guard myself, never knowing if it would be lips or teeth, ratcheted me up to a point where I was breathless and wild beneath him.

"Jesus, Ace. Your pussy...heaven," he said right in my ear. "I could fuck you all night," he said and then he bit my neck just above my thrumming pulse.

I came. With no precursor or warning. The words and the small burst of pain did me in. I said, "Oh, Charlie" and then came. My back arched and my breath left me.

Charlie shook his head, chewed his lower lip. He laughed softly, said, "Ace, what am I gonna do with you?" And then he was coming, head bowed, arms shaking with the force of it.

I surprised us both by bursting into tears.

CHAPTER EIGHT

Charlie froze and I felt so bad for startling him. But then he dropped to the bed next to me, pulled me into his arms and began to stroke my hair. "What's going on in that head of yours, Abby?"

I shuddered, more mortified than upset now. "I am so *so* sorry." My words stumbled over each other, my tongue tripping over itself. "I have no idea—" I shrugged. "I just think it's been so long and—"

He smiled down at me and kissed my fingers. "Sex can be emotional. I am choosing to see this as a compliment."

I laughed, my whole body shook with sudden amusement. And I found that I didn't care. I didn't care that my breasts weren't as perfect as they'd been when I was twenty. Or that I had that small belly pooch that short of an electric carving knife or plastic surgery I couldn't afford was never going away. Or that I had small lines around my mouth and something weird was beginning with my neck. I didn't care because when I was with him I felt so damn beautiful. So *wanted* that I felt like I had nothing to worry about.

To Charlie I was beautiful and in that moment I was even more beautiful to myself.

"And brave," I whispered, not meaning to say it aloud.

"And brave what?" He stroked my hair, still damp from my preparatory shower.

"To sleep with you," I said. Then I laughed at the shocked look on his face.

"Am I that beastly?" he asked, trying to keep a straight face.

"No!" I squeaked, swatting his chest playfully. "What I mean is, it can be daunting. Someone like you."

"Like what?"

"Someone as young and handsome and fucking…buff," I said.

Charlie played along by flexing his biceps to make me laugh again. "I'm Hans…" he started, reviving an old Saturday Night Live skit. At his age God only knows where he'd seen it. Probably Youtube.

I craned my neck up and kissed him quiet. "You know what I mean, Charlie," I said. "To you this might make perfect sense. It seems to."

He watched me, finger skating along my bare hip raising up goose bumps as he stroked. He didn't try to cut me off, just kept his mouth shut and waited.

"But for me, I kind of shake my head sometimes and wonder how I got here." I smoothed my hands along his chest just to feel his warm, supple skin. "I was considering an online profile for people over forty just a week ago." I snorted and that made me freeze and then giggle. He smiled. "And now…I'm having amazing spontaneous take-me-now sex with you."

"Hans," he said, managing to keep a straight face.

I shook my head. "Just Charlie. Charlie who makes me smile."

"And let's not forget orgasms," he whispered. His lips tickled along my shoulder and in that second all I could feel was blood throbbing beneath the places on my skin where he'd used his teeth.

"How could I forget those?" I was growing wet and ready again. My heart rate picking up, my head becoming muzzy.

"I have an important question, Abby."

"What's that?"

"Is there food? Because," he said, rolling atop me. His weight settling on me. It was a welcome, wonderful sensation. "I could have sworn when I came in I smelled food. But you..." His hand slipped up the inside of my thigh. His thumb nudged the crook of my thigh but he didn't touch me where I wanted. He touched me everywhere but.

Until I panted, "I?"

"You were too damn enticing to worry about food." His stomach rumbled and he cocked an eyebrow at me. I laughed so hard it shook us both. "But now my stomach seems to be demanding some payment.'"

"There is food," I said. "Horrible, junky, fried greasy food."

He pretended surprise. "My favorite kind! And there's a rumor of whiskey too."

"Hot toddies," I corrected.

He kissed me softly and I parted my lips to allow his tongue inside to war with mine. When he broke the kiss he whispered against my ear. "Hot toddies in bed. Because you require zinc."

I rolled my eyes, smiling

"Which means you need my constant attention and care

in this bed so that you recover from your…"

"Imaginary cold?"

"Yes, that," Charlie said. "I hear those are dangerous."

He got up, pulled me to my feet and proceeded to walk bare-assed toward my kitchen. I couldn't help but stand there and admire the view.

*

"This is some of the best bad food I've ever had," Charlie said.

We were camped out in my bed with a movie going in the background. It was fully dark outside and sleet ticked against the window. Somehow I found the whole scene very cozy and reassuring. And that made me a little nervous.

"Yeah, they make a killer mozzarella stick."

"And you had to go and ruin it with salad," he scoffed.

"This 'salad' has more meat, cheese and egg in it than salad!" I said. "Which I think means it fits just fine in that 'bad food' category."

"Okay, okay if you say so." Charlie stole a hunk of salami and cheese, eating it with his fingers. He licked them one by one as he watched me.

I found myself a little breathless, watching that tongue peek out over and over. "When did you want the toddies?" I said, my voice giving my arousal away.

I could tell because when he smiled it was that crooked bad boy half smile. "Oh, later. Right now I want something else." When he gathered our paper plates and takeout stuff and put it all on my bedside table, I simply watched, as a steady pounding pulse beat between my legs.

"What?" I breathed.

"You."

"Again?"

"Again," he said, pushing me back. "And again…and again…" His hands parted my thighs and I chewed my lower lip. I knew what I hoped he was going to do. I had no idea if he'd do it.

He kissed up my inner thighs, his lips a whisper on that tender, soft skin. My entire body flustered at it. I realized I was holding my breath when tiny white sparkles appeared in my vision. I exhaled before drawing in a deep breath. It seemed to be what he was waiting for, because when I took in that air, he parted my nether lips with his tongue, nudging my clitoris with just the right amount of pressure to cause me to cry out.

"Shh, pretty lady," he said. He did it again and my hips arched up, seeking the wet heat of his tongue even though it felt nearly overwhelming. Charlie splayed his hands on my upper thighs. Pressed down. Tethered me to earth so I didn't float away.

His mouth covered me and he sucked with small even bursts so that my clit throbbed with blood, my limbs heavy with lust and pleasure.

Just as I got used to that rhythm he changed it. Swirling patterns along my sensitive flesh until I wriggled, then he moved to broad even licks. All the while his fingers swept back and forth along the tops of my thighs. I was holding my breath again and my head felt swimmy from it. But it added a fuzzy, pleasant lethargy to the moment.

When Charlie pushed his fingers inside me and raked his teeth gently over my clit, my outer lips, and even my mound, I spiraled down into a flurry of sensations.

I came, my hips slamming up fast and hard. Hard enough that even he couldn't still me. "Jesus Christ," I whispered, shaking with the force of my orgasm.

"Nope. Still me. Hans," he chuckled.

"I can't…I mean…" I shook my head, trying to breathe deeply. "Just wow."

"Just wow," he echoed. His fingers were still in me and he nudged my tight internal muscles so that a slow ribbon of pleasure unfurled inside me. An aftershock.

Once I caught my breath and my heart slowed, I turned to him. "How's that whiskey sounding?" I asked.

He sat up and kissed me. His mouth tasted like me and I realized I relished it.

"Whiskey's sounding good," he said. "Everything you say sounds good," he said. "Especially, *Oh, Charlie! Charlie you're a sex god!*" He said the last in a fairly convincing falsetto until I was laughing out loud.

"Is that what I sound like?"

"Nah. But a guy can dream. I've always wanted to be a sex god."

"Don't worry," I said, kissing his knuckles. "You are."

We'd fallen into an easy relationship. We got along. We joked. We were definitely sexually compatible and then some. I realized as I threw on my robe and led him to the kitchen that I was scared. I wasn't sure yet if it was in a good or a bad way.

*

He stood near me at the counter, wearing just his jeans. Charlie in nothing but jeans was a distracting sight. Bare feet, bare chest, bare arms. I realized he didn't have a single tattoo. Nowadays that seemed downright odd within his age group.

"No tats," I said. Even Heath had a tattoo of a thunderbird on his shoulder. Rose was talking about a crow on her wrist. I'd even considered one.

He shrugged, touching me briefly as I moved past him to the spice cabinet to gather cloves, nutmeg and cinnamon sticks.

"Just haven't found anything I want to wear on my skin until I die," he said.

I nodded. "Me too. I've thought about it. Since I turned thirty actually. My kids tease me that I'm a chicken, but really, I just want something that I still like every day that I look at it. I haven't found that thing yet." I looked past him and realized I'd forgotten something. "Honey," I said pointing.

"I prefer if you call me darling," Charlie said and then kissed me.

I couldn't help but laugh, the man made me happy. "I meant can you hand me the honey," I said. "Or I'm never going to get this drink made!"

He pinned me to the counter briefly by placing a hand on either side and caging me between his arms. "Kiss me and I'll get it."

I kissed him. Reaching up to loop my arms around his neck. My robe gaped open just enough that when I pressed against him slightly, I felt my breast flatten against the hot expanse of his bare chest. He generated heat like a human furnace.

When I broke the kiss, I gasped, "Honey?"

"Coming up, baby," he said, winking.

I put the water on to boil and said, "Squeeze about a teaspoon in each mug," I said.

He did and then dropped a cinnamon stick in each mug. "Where's the booze, Ace?"

"In my bedroom closet," I said.

He cocked an eyebrow and grinned. "What? Why? Closet drinker?"

I snorted. "I used to keep it in there when the kids were growing up instead of down in the house. Just because I worried. So if you opened the closet you'd see my clothes, Jack's clothes…" I stumbled over that part a little. It was the first I'd mentioned my ex to Charlie. "And a liquor cabinet. I still get teased over that."

"Be right back," he said.

I took a breath while he was gone. Inhaling deeply, clearing my head. He made my mind muddy and my body hungry. I found that I was rather proud of myself for being so okay in my skin. I, in fact, found I felt more okay in my skin then I had in a long time.

"It's only a fling," I said. "Nothing to be afraid of."

I heard him come up behind me just then and wondered if he heard me. I turned, preparing myself to explain, but he simply sauntered in the room and then set the whiskey bottle down. "I see you appreciate the good stuff."

"Always," I said, kissing him yet again. It never got old, the kissing. I felt bad for my comment, though. Not that I didn't mean what I said but if he'd heard me it could have hurt his feelings. No one likes to be told they're just a temporary placeholder. A way for someone to get their feet wet.

Besides, Charlie would tire of me and move on to a girl his age. I'd be a fool if I didn't see the situation for what it was. And the one thing a failed marriage and two teens had taught me was to always see the situation as it really was.

CHAPTER NINE

Hot toddies turned to slow kissing. Then a long hot shower. We finished the rest of the cold leftovers and then sat on the sofa like two fat bears after a long hibernation.

"So tell me about your kids," Charlie said, taking my foot in his hand and rubbing my instep.

I moaned as if we were in the middle of stellar sex, which was how good it felt. When I finally found my voice, I said, "Rose is my baby, she's the youngest twin. She's gorgeous and quiet and thoughtful and fiercely smart. Rose is in her first year at Frostburg. She's not sure what she wants to do but she is focusing primarily, at the moment, on English Lit."

He nodded. "Nice. I once considered writing the great American novel." His fingertips walked along the ball of my foot and I let out a sigh that was almost embarrassing.

"Haven't we all," I laughed. "She thinks she might want to be a teacher someday. However, I've read her creative writing and she is highly capable. I think she could give writing a run for its money if she decided to."

"And your son?"

"My Heath," I laughed. "He's funny and handsome and kind hearted. He's in the Marines. He decided he couldn't find a direction. School wasn't so much his thing, so he joined the military. As a way to help find himself, he said. I couldn't argue. My father did the same once upon a time, learned to weld, built a family and turned out great. So…I worry."

"Of course," he said. Then he leaned over and kissed my hip. Nothing more, nothing less. Then he took my other foot and began to give it the same mind melting attention. I was in heaven.

"I miss them. Terribly. But it makes me wonderfully happy that they are out there beginning to stake claim to their own lives, you know?"

"It means you did your job," he said.

I felt my face color but not because of sexiness or touching or arousal. It colored because he'd just nailed it. He got it. I took pride in my kids because I'd loved them so hard and put so much energy and thought into their raising, that I felt pride at the people they were today.

"Thank you for getting that," I said softly. Then: "What about you and your mom? You get along?"

Charlie nodded. "We did. I lost her when I was about your kids' age. Breast cancer."

My heart plummeted. "Oh, Charlie. I'm sorry." I tried to withdraw my foot but he held it tight, kept rubbing.

"It's okay, Ace. I've had years to adjust. And I feel lucky…" He rubbed his knuckles along my instep and my entire body felt warm and pliable. "I had her for nineteen years. I was best friends with a boy in middle school whose dad died the year he was born. He never knew his dad. Had no memories. Me…I have tons of them. Good ones." His fingers worked up my calf and I realized I was holding my breath, listening to him. Getting a glimpse of what was inside of goodhearted, kind, handsome Charlie. "I had nineteen years when I was told every day with words or without that I was loved. Loved beyond a doubt."

I swallowed hard against tears that wanted to come. Instead, I wiggled my foot in his grip and let my head fall back on the sofa. I listened to the sleet and the steady sound of his breathing. Fifteen or twenty minutes ticked by and I was boneless from his touch. When I raised my head he was watching me, smiling.

"What?"

"Nothing," he said, his smile growing bigger. "You're just so damn pretty."

I pulled my foot from his hand because he wasn't anticipating it. I got up on my knees, leaned over him to kiss him. His hands curled to my waist, stroking slowly against my robe. Excitement coiled through me and I pulled at the buttons of his fly. I freed his cock, thumbing the tip, giving him a few good strokes. When his hips arched up, I tugged the jeans down. I got on my knees and pushed between his splayed legs.

He didn't say a word, just watched me in the low light of the single lamp of the room. He kept his hands on his thighs and his eyes on me. I slipped the head of his cock into my mouth, ran my tongue along the silken rim, slithered it over the divot in the top. I tasted the salty-sweetness of pre-come. When his eyes drifted shut a pounding arousal filled me. It was the intoxicating feeling of power. Nothing was as powerful as bringing another person pleasure. Nothing was as wonderful.

I stroked him, sucking the tip, sliding my open mouth down one side of his shaft only to come up the other. I'd forgotten the intimacy of a blow job. How it could be so intimate it made your throat tight. Which was what I was experiencing. The slam of power and emotion.

Slipping my lips as low as I could, I stroked his balls in unison with the motion of my mouth. "Jesus…Abby," he said. My eyes were closed but he sounded like he was smiling.

I didn't answer him. I didn't want to banter, I wanted him to come.

When his hips became a steady desperate rhythm, raising up in short bursts, I sped up. I sucked harder, lapped at him with my tongue, wrapped my hand around him and found a steady beat of strokes.

His fingers twined in my still-damp hair, tugging so that I hissed but kept going. I felt the sexual thrill of that moment in the pit of my stomach, in the pulse in my pussy. My gasp was as loud as Charlie's when he came. I pulled back, moving so I could paint my lower lips, my chest, and my hair with his come. My hand continuing to slide up and down his cock until his head was tilted back, his breathing fast, and laughter was shaking him.

"Now what is so funny, Charlie?"

"Nothing." He craned his neck to look at me. He brushed the hair out of my face. Then looked at his fingers, sticky with come. He ran his finger along my lower lip, spreading the salty fluid like lipstick, then sat up to touch the wetness on my chest. "Jesus, that's sexy."

"I have to work up to swallowing," I said, feeling heat in my cheeks. I glanced down. "It's been a *really* long time since I've done that."

He nodded and leaned in to kiss me. Which surprised me. The kiss deepened and I found his willingness to kiss me while my lips were glossed in his come the sexiest thing I could imagine.

"Thank you, Abby," he said.

I blinked. "For what?"

"For that. I imagine that's more sacred to you than sex."

Sacred. Yes. He'd nailed it. Again. He seemed to have the ability to look into my head. And it frightened me just enough to still the breath in my lungs.

"It is," I admitted.

He nodded. "I get it."

He kissed me again. "I should go."

Desire and relief twisted inside my chest. I wanted him to stay. I was relieved he was leaving. The intimacy level had soared in a few short days. I was amazed by it but also terrified. I wasn't sure *how* I felt about Charlie or how fast things were happening.

"I...it's late," I said.

A few minutes later we stood at the door, Charlie fully dressed with his coat on. He pulled me in for a hug. "What about tomorrow, Ace? Can I see you? We could finally give that tapas place a try."

I lied. In a heartbeat. Before I could even think of it. And it startled me. "I can't. I have a late meeting and then have to bring some work home with me. It's important." I kissed him, feeling like an asshole and hiding it to the best of my ability. "I'm sorry."

"How about the next night then?" He grinned. "There's a party. Next block over from my house. My friend Ken's new place. Come with me. Party with me, Abby."

I wanted to say no but the look on his face said it was important. And surely I'd only need the one night to have a breather. It's not like we were engaged. We were having an affair. We were sleeping together. We were having fun.

"Sure," I said though anxiety flooded me even as I said it. "Sounds like fun."

When I shut the door I had a moment of horrible guilt. I'd lied to Charlie. Why had I done that? What was the point?

"The point is too much too fast," I said to Elliot. Who promptly blinked at me with his auburn gaze, swished his fat fluffy tail and turned around and walked away. "Thanks for the input," I called after him.

*

The workday dragged. I got a few texts from Charlie but only answered one or two. I wanted the illusion of busyness to feel real. I answered his one text about Friday with fake excitement and a smiley face. The truth was, I was terrified to attend a party with his friends. I was worried to the point of a sick stomach about what his peers would think. I chewed ginger chews all day to keep the queasiness at bay. And when Cathleen asked me if the zinc was working I nearly punched her in the face because, to me, zinc had become code for sleeping with Charlie.

When I finally got in my car to go home I was on the verge of weeping with relief. When my cell rang, my blood turned to ice in my veins. I glanced at the read out and let out a hearty sigh when I saw LOUISE THE GREAT on the screen.

"Yes," I said.

"Well, that's rude. Hello, is better. Or Abby Marsh's phone. Or even, this is the tart sleeping with a young stud, would work."

"Louise!" I barked.

"Okay, okay, jeesh. Don't joke with Abby. What's wrong with you? I'd think you'd be more even keeled with all the vigorous young person sexy time."

"Jesus," I sighed. "Louise!"

She sighed back and I almost smiled. "Where are you?"

"Just leaving work."

"Meet me at Donovan's. We'll eat. We'll drink. You'll confide in me. It will be like a movie."

"I can't."

"You can."

"I can't!" I was lying.

"You're lying," she said. I sighed again and Louise laughed "We've been friends since forever, I know when you're lying, Abby. Now meet me. I'm on my way now." Then she hung up leaving me only two options. Obey or stand her up.

"God damn it," I said, and then I put the car in gear. I guess I was eating dinner at Donovan's.

Donovan's wasn't packed yet, which was nice. I found Louise at a table with a pitcher of amber ale and a plate of loaded potato skins. "Skins and then more sins," she said when I sat down.

"My cholesterol just went up," I said looking at the cheese and bacon and sour cream.

"Oh come on! You're sucking up vicarious youth. Surely this cholesterol is nothing for your young, rejuvenated system." She dumped a potato skin on my plate and poured me a beer.

"What are the other sins? Dare I ask?"

"Well, I was thinking after these we can split a lobster roll. They're the special tonight and you know they're huge and buttery." She sipped her beer. "And decadent."

I took a bite of my potato skin, rolled my eyes, groaned and nodded. "Yes, yes," I said.

"Shouldn't you be saying that in bed with Charlie?"

I shut my eyes and shook my head. When I opened my eyes she was watching me in that way she has that feels more like being X-rayed than looked at.

"What?" I said, taking another bite of my pre-dinner junk food.

"What's wrong?" she asked.

"Nothing!"

Louise rolled her eyes. "What's *wrong*?"

"Nothing…"

She stared at me.

I swallowed hard. Tried not to cave. I failed. "I…" I shook my head again. "Never mind."

"What is wroooooooong!" Louise said a bit too loud.

I leaned in and hushed her when a few people glanced our way. "Hush or I'm going to cut you off!"

"You can't cut me off because I bought the beer. And the food! And you're lying to me, best friend. So please, save us all a bunch of back and forth and just tell me what's wrong."

"I like him," I said.

"Oh, how terrible." She frowned at me and ate a piece of bacon off her plate.

I groaned and put my head in my hands long enough to draw a deep breath and collect my thoughts. Then I returned to my amber ale. "I like him more than I should for a fling. And that's all this is. A fling."

"Try to think of him as a young friend you bang."

I choked on beer and felt it sting the inside of my nose. "Louise!"

"It works. I had a little…" she shrugged. "Thing, when Tom and I split up. It was very brief."

"So brief you never told me!" I said.

"Yes. That brief. It was only a few times. We laughed, we

ate, we drank, we fucked and then we were over it. He was the guy who fixed copy machines in offices when they broke. He came in one day, he came a few times with me..." She snorted. "And then we were done. He was twenty-three or four, I think. We got along well in and out of bed but there was no way it was going to last any longer. No way."

"Right! But I really get along with Charlie and—"

"It's normal," she said.

"What's normal?"

"Getting attached to the first guy you've been with after a long commitment. You and Jack were together twenty years. That's a long-ass time."

"Tell me about it," I said.

"And now there's this new guy who makes your blood flow faster, he's nice, *and* he's good in the sack judging by the rosy glow of your cheeks, my friend. And you like him. So in your romantic brain there's more to it than compatibility. But there's not. And as time goes on, you'll realize that and relax."

"Yeah?" I asked, hoping she was right.

"Yeah."

"Good," I sighed. "I was really worried. And I'm supposed to go to a party with him tomorrow."

"Don't worry. Go party! You're smart. You know deep down that this is just an affair." She pointed at me. "And how exciting is that? An affair!"

I laughed and nodded. I had to agree. I finished off another potato skin as she ordered our meal. When I left Donovan's my pants felt too tight, my head a tiny bit buzzed, but I was much more relaxed than when I entered.

Sommer Marsden

CHAPTER TEN

"Hi," he said. God he looked good. Dark wash jeans and a button down olive green shirt. He had on a knit tie and a cardigan. The effect should have been grandpa but it wasn't. It was sexy. I looked at his feet.

"Desert boots," I said.

Charlie looked down at his feet. "Yeah. You don't like them?"

I shook my head, laughed. "No, I do like them, but they're updated."

He stuck his foot out, turned his ankle and examined his own shoes. "Updated?"

"They had desert boots when I was a kid. They were squarish and ugly and had booger bottoms."

Charlie laughed. "Booger bottoms?"

I bent to look at the rubber gum sole of his shoes. "Yep. Same bottoms. Only the ones in the 70s were thicker. You could tear off a little piece, roll it up like a…" I stumbled on my own words.

"Booger?" he snorted.

"Well, yeah." I smiled. "And throw them or even flick them at people." I straightened up as a cold wind blew heard enough to chill me through my coat.

"Sounds like fun."

"Well, you know, we didn't have the internet then." That earned me a laugh. "I never wore them. I hated them. But I do recognize them."

"Did you want to come in or go right to the party?"

If I went in his apartment we'd end up in bed. There was no doubt about it. And I wasn't sure if I was ready for that today. I was still reeling from how easy things seemed to be with Charlie. Beyond the bedroom. In the bedroom things went so well I forgot to worry. Which was possibly what I needed but…

"Let's just go," I said. "You said we can walk?"

Charlie pulled the door shut and locked it. Then he took my arm and kissed me. The kiss was warm and soft and toe curling. "Yep. Right around the corner…but I'm in no hurry."

He took my gloved hand and squeezed.

"Why's that?"

"I didn't get to see you yesterday. I want to soak you up before I have to share you."

The wind blew again and I shivered. "Well, here I am. Soak away," I joked.

We walked hand in hand toward the party that terrified me. A crowd of kids his age. And in a group that's what they were to me. Kids. I knew Charlie was a grown man. I knew he was an adult. But I couldn't help but feel like the mother walking into a frat party.

Part of that was my perception. It was skewed if not downright judgmental.

"Should I have brought wine or something?" I asked,

suddenly panicky about my lack of adult beverage to donate to the cause.

"Nah. I gave Ken money for the keg. It covers me and you. And I have a feeling you can't drink a whole lot of beer."

"I'm about a two or three beer person."

"Yeah, I figured."

I laughed. "What's that supposed to mean?"

"Beer bloats," he said, shrugging. "At least that's what all the girlfriends say."

"The girlfriends?"

"You'll meet most of them tonight. There's Ken's girlfriend, Dan's, Kendall's. The other guys probably have a girl along. Someone they're dating. But they always complain, "beer bloats you…"" he did his girl falsetto again, making me laugh.

I paused to stare at the sky. It was clear. No snow or sleet threatening. In the navy blue darkness were pinpricks of white light and a sliver of moon.

"You okay?"

"The truth?"

"Yes," he said, squeezing my hand again. "Of course."

"I'm terrified."

"Why?"

"Your friends." I shrugged. "I'm just nervous. I'm different."

"You're awesome."

"To you," I said. But then: "Let's go. I'm being a baby. Let's just go." I pulled him along. "I'm fine."

"We don't have to—"

"No," I said. "We can't tuck ourselves away in apartments and never go out."

"Right," he said nodding. "I want to show my girlfriend off."

My heart stuttered. I felt, despite the cold, a thin film of sweat along my upper lip. I was horrified but did my best not to react and keep walking. I sucked in a big breath of air trying to regulate my heart. I was horrified that he thought I was his girlfriend after just a week. I was also horrified that the moment he said it, I felt a leap of happiness in my blood. How stupid and dangerous would that be? To actually get *involved* with Charlie.

Stupid and dangerous beyond words.

I looked at him, happy in the white glow from the streetlights. I'd talk to him about it later. After the party we'd sit down and I'd let him know what this was. Just a fling.

*

The house was packed. I was instantly transported back to the block parties we used to have when the kids were small. We'd go from house to house, often spilling over into the yard even in chillier weather. People kept their kids in tow so even if someone got tipsy there was no driving to factor in. It had been good, drunken, low budget fun. And this party was the same.

We were just getting our beers and I'd met Ken and two other friends, I was already having trouble keeping track of names in the chaos, when the power went out.

"You know what that means!" Ken shouted.

"Bail team!" a bunch of people yelled.

"Bail team?" I asked.

"We take turns bailing out the sump pump when it fills until the power comes back on."

I blinked at him. "But it's winter," I said softly. Way too softly for the noise that was going on in here.

"Ken's house is built on wet property," Charlie said.

"A freaking underground stream," Ken said, walking past with a stack of red Solo cups. "That damn sump pump runs all day even in a drought. So, that's why I'm glad all you sorry sons of bitches happened to be here when it shit the bed."

His eyes drifted to me and then Ken said, "Erm, sorry…"

I shrugged, suddenly feeling like someone's grandmother. The moment they felt they had to watch their behavior or language around me was the moment it was confirmed I was the outcast.

I was now the outcast.

"Let me introduce you to the girls." Ken tugged me along and brought me to a stop at a flock of beautiful young women. Three to be exact. Their eyes turned to me all at once and I felt like the ugly duckling walking into the cool kids section of the cafeteria. How a grown woman can go from forty-two to sixteen in a split second is beyond me.

Knock it off. You're a grownup and so are they.

I forced myself to put my shoulders back, stand up straight, smile and above all else breathe.

"Ladies, this is Charlie's date, Abby. Abby, this is my girlfriend Beverly." The long legged, brunet with startling blue eyes nodded. She was decked out in skinny jeans, ankle boots and a gray sweater that played up those eyes to perfection.

She smiled at me but the smile didn't touch her eyes. "And this is Dan's girl Angie. And here we have Shea, Kendall's girlfriend." The two blondes turned to eye me up. Both gave equally stiff smiles and they muttered "hi".

"I'm taking Charlie boy down to bail first. Otherwise I won't get a day's work out of him," Ken said.

Charlie had found us and he gave me a reassuring smile. "I'll be right back."

I could feel the three witches—I mean girls—watching me and I had to think fast. "Do you mind showing me to the powder room before you go?"

One of the girls slid her eyes my way and I held my breath when she said, "Oh, I can show her, Charlie."

Charlie felt my arm go tense. I'd looped it through his just for the contact. I hated this. Hated feeling out of place. Hated feeling desperate not to be alone with people. I'd conquered my mild social anxiety years ago. When you have young kids you can't be shy. But this—this was worse than anything I'd ever encountered. I felt ready to bolt like a frightened horse.

"That's okay, Bev. It's on the way." He maneuvered me through the candle and flashlight lit home. People banged into us, some laughing too hard, some caught in quiet conversation.

"Please don't leave me," I said. I felt my face grow hot and red with blush. Thank God he couldn't see.

We stopped in front of the bathroom. Someone had thought to put a tall sconce with a candle inside on the sink. That way no one would drown in the toilet.

"It's fine. I promise. I'll go bail." He waved his Solo cup and laughed. "Take my turn, do my duty and come rescue you. Then we can find a dark corner and make out. It'll be really dirty and fun."

I laughed. I couldn't help myself. That part of the scenario sounded nice. The part where he'd go bail and leave me up here, not so much. I sighed. "I'll be fine. I'm being a baby."

He hugged me, kissed me once on the lips while someone by the basement steps yelled, "Charlie! No escaping your man-duty, dude!"

"I'll be right back, Ace. Promise."

"I'll be fine," I said, lying full-on to his face.

I went to the bathroom, watched myself in the large vanity mirror as I washed my hands. I looked younger in the candlelight. Maybe I could carry a candle around on all my dates with Charlie.

Tears pricked my eyes. "Stop the pity party, Ace," I said to myself in the mirror. The crazy yellow-orange flickering glow matched how tumultuous I felt inside. "You're a grown woman who should be able to stand with a handful of twenty-somethings and have a conversation. Even if you're faking it."

Instead of leaving, I sat on the edge of the tub and tried to let time pass. So what if they thought I'd died in here? So what if I'd told Charlie I'd try and have fun but instead had tucked myself away from the party? So what?

Someone banged on the door and I jumped. I glanced at my phone's illuminated screen. Only about ten minutes had passed but it was long enough that people were probably waiting to come in.

"Yo! Someone needs to get in there!" the mystery person called.

"Coming!" I yelled. I stood, inhaled deeply and opened the door.

A guy with his cap on backwards ushered a girl inside. She wasn't looking too steady on her feet and judging by the way she lurched toward the toilet, she wasn't feeling too steady either. I managed to slip out the door before the retching began.

Since it was dark and only lit by splashes of orange candle glow or stark white flashlight illumination, I seemed to ping-pong from cluster of people to cluster of people. I took a left thinking I'd find the girls again—not that I was in any hurry to see them, but instead I found myself by the front door. I overheard someone say, "…as old as my mom. At least."

I turned on my heels and tried the opposite direction.

They're not necessarily talking about you. I tried to talk myself down but I wasn't buying it. Who else would they be talking about? I hadn't seen any other forty-somethings here at this noisy house party. Just me and a bunch of kids.

Someone had started a fire in the fireplace and it illuminated the trio in the center of the room. They hadn't budged. None of them saw me coming. None of them were paying attention to anything other than the topic that amused them so.

Beverly said, "What's the opposite of robbing the cradle? Robbing the grave?" Then she laughed her mean girl laugh.

Angie leaned in and touched her shoulder in total agreement. "I mean really, what was Charlie thinking?"

The third one—whose name I'd already forgotten—said, "She must be a stellar lay."

Beverly chimed in, giddy with cattiness. "Maybe when she takes her teeth out she gives a hell of a blow job."

I didn't intend to make a noise. But I must have made a noise, because they suddenly turned my way simultaneously as if they were one giant bitchy-girl organism. Beverly said, "Shit" just as someone started clapping and whooping loudly in the dark and I jumped.

I turned to leave. Not run. Fuck them if I'd run. But I was done. I'd text Charlie that I had to go. That I didn't feel well. Because I didn't. The little bit of beer I had consumed roiled in my stomach like something toxic. I realized the drum beat sound I was hearing as my own heart and I then realized I was having an anxiety attack. And I hated that more than anything. That I'd let these girls—children really—make me feel this way. I was allowing this bullshit, I thought, as my feet hurried toward the place I thought the front door to be.

Adrenaline sharpened my hearing but not my sight. I ran face first into Charlie who caught my upper shoulders and stilled me. "Hey, what—"

Then he caught on, looked up in the direction of the gaggle where Ken already stood frowning. "We didn't say anything that wasn't true," Beverly said to him but loudly enough for me to hear.

"I mean, she is *old*," Angie said in a faux whisper.

Just then the lights decided to pop on to spotlight my horror and shame. Most of the oblivious crowd cheered. "Jesus Christ," Charlie said, real anger burning in his eyes as he looked at his friends.

"Hey man, sorry," Ken said. But he didn't say a word to me. "I mean—"

Charlie held up his hand. "Don't finish that sentence."

I pulled free, done with standing there being a spectacle. "I have to go," I said. Thank God my coat was on a peg by the front door and I hadn't brought a bag. I hurried outside into the cold air and sucked in a great frigid breath to try and wash away the racing anxiety in my gut.

I heard Charlie call out to me, "Abby!" but I was already walking.

I heard him call "Jesus Christ, you assholes. What's *wrong* with you?" as he left. But even that was not enough to slow me down. I walked toward his house where my car was. I'd get in my car. Go home. Crawl into bed and sleep. For the weekend.

I started to run and didn't know why until I realized that I could hear his feet pounding toward me. By the time I reached the end of his road, I felt sick from pushing my body so fast, sucking in cold air as I ran.

He caught my arm, "Abby!" but when I pulled free of him he let me go. Not holding onto me against my will. "Abby, please talk to me," he said.

I shook my head. Tears flowing freely then. Which made me so ashamed. That I would let them get to me like that. That I'd let them manipulate my emotions with their petty cruelty.

I used my key fob to unlock my car, the lights flashing a welcome. Charlie was right behind me but I refused to look at him.

When I opened the door, he touched my arm. That was all. Just a touch. To his credit, again, he didn't grab me. "Please, Abby, you're not being fair. I'm not my friends. They don't speak for me—fuck, they can barely speak for themselves! I'm not their stupid senses of humor or their narrow-minded bullshit. I'm me."

"Let go, Charlie," I said softly. He did, immediately. Part of me wished he hadn't. My heart fell a little, but I got in the car. "Go home, Charlie."

"Abby, listen to me. Most of them were drunk. I didn't tell them anything about you because I thought it was irrelevant."

"They didn't think it was irrelevant."

"Apparently, they're bigger idiots than I thought!" he roared

"This has been my fear, Charlie. It was fine as sex. As a…fling. But I can't be anything more than that. I can't be your…anything. It won't work."

"You're letting them decide that for you?" he asked, his jaw tense in the bright streetlights.

"No. I'm deciding it," I said. "For me." I started the car.

"Abby, come on. This is stupid. Things are good. It's been a hell of a week." He grinned at me and it broke my heart. When he saw my expression, the grin fell away. "Abby."

"Go home, Charlie," I said again. "We're done. I'm sorry."

I pulled the door shut before he could stop me and drove home. Oddly, I felt fine driving home. But when I got home and pulled the fridge door open to find two lonely chicken wings wrapped in takeout paper I burst into tears. Lovely.

CHAPTER ELEVEN

Saturday was a blur of self-pity. Instead of emotional eating, I did the exact opposite. I had no appetite for any food. If anything, I craved cigarettes which I'd stopped smoking, thank you very much. Saturday night, while I attempted to watch a movie, I finally turned my phone off from the texts and calls. I knew he was right, I wasn't being fair to him, but I couldn't seem to escape what felt like certainty that one day he'd feel the same as his friends had. Even one day soon.

Sunday morning, I woke to hear someone banging on the door. My heart was conflicted. Part of me hoped it was him, part of me feared it. I was standing in the foyer, realizing I hadn't gotten dressed all weekend and that my hair was standing on end when I heard "Let me in or I'm going to call the police and tell them I'm afraid you died and Elliot ate you!"

Elliot, upon hearing his name, jumped down off the radiator and sauntered off with a fuck-you look.

"Louise," I hissed.

I tied my robe, ran my hands through my hair and realized it was hopeless. Utterly hopeless. She'd take one look at me and know I was having a pity party.

"Did he? Did Elliot eat you?" she yelled.

"No!" I barked, stomping to the door. "Elliot did not eat me. He's left me in peace. You know, using this thing called *courtesy*."

She barged in with a bag of food and a box of wine. "Oooh, the cat has courtesy. Lucky you. Listen, if you prefer a life with no best friend who doesn't care about you and love you and worry about you and all that I can totally just g—"

"Oh, shut up," I sighed. "Get in here. The wind is cold."

"Yeah, no shit! I've been standing out there because *someone* wouldn't let me in. I have food," she said, shaking the bag at me.

"Not hungry."

"Not even for Mickeys' burgers?"

"Nope."

"Hunh. I got you the Mickey belly buster extra pickles. I figured you hadn't eaten—"

My stomach growled desperately and she smirked at me. "You might not be hungry but your gut is. There's also wine."

"No wine."

"No burgers, no wine. Who are you? Are you a pod person?" she pushed past me and began to spread the food out on the table.

"No. I'm fine."

"You're not fine. Your heart is broken."

"You have to be in love to have your heart broken," I said.

"No," she leveled a finger at me. "You can be *falling* in love and have your heart broken."

"I was not falling in love," I said. I picked at a thread on my robe.

"You sure?"

"I'm sure. I only knew him a week."

"Liar," she said. "And time is negligible when you make a connection with someone."

I sat at the table and opened my burger. I pulled all the sesame seeds off the bun as she began to eat. "I was not falling in love."

"Oh, I think you were. Even just a little. But it scared the shit out of you. An affair itself scared the shit out of you but the love part was too much."

"I was not falling in love!" I threw a sesame seed at her and it bounced off her chin. A wild little giggle burst out of me.

"M'kay," she muttered, wiping her face. "If you say so."

"I say so."

"But I've seen you in love. More than once. And it was a pretty spot on impersonation."

"You didn't say that the other day with your whole fling speech," I whispered.

She raised an eyebrow. "I wasn't going to bet the one to tell you something like that."

I sighed and started to shred the bun. She smacked my hand lightly. "Jesus, what are you a squirrel? Eat it, don't disassemble it."

"I'm not hungry."

"How many times has he called you?" she asked.

"Seven. Seven phone calls and six texts. I turned the phone off. There could be more."

"There are more," she said. "Now tell me what happened. Because you were enjoying the sex and him and doing a really good job of focusing on the sex and not the little flickers of really liking him you were feeling."

"Louise…"

"Oh for God's sake, we both know you're going to tell me. So can you just tell me right out of the gate?"

"Bleh," I said.

She laughed, eating another bite of her burger. Then she found us some glasses and poured out wine. When I was holding the striped wine glass I loved the most, I ate a fry and sighed again.

"Spill."

So I told her the whole sordid tale. Told her about Beverly and Angie and the third nameless girl. Told her how it made me feel—hollowed out, empty, less than. How Charlie had reacted and what I'd said to him and all the mopey bullshit since then.

"So you did to Charlie the very thing you rage against most," she said succinctly, finishing her burger and washing it down with cheap wine.

"What?" But as soon as she said it I felt my stomach drop with dread.

She waved a finger at me and said, "When the kids were little, you used to give them shit if they judged one person on the actions of another. It happened more than once. I can still hear you saying that you have to judge each person on their own actions and intentions."

I swallowed hard, feeling like a heel. I felt every moment of my wallowing weekend and ran a hand through my messed up dirty hair. Ugh.

"Did he take you there with the intention of you being hurt?"

I sighed. "No…" I drew the word out very much like a surly teenager.

"And did he say or do any of those things that hurt you so much and put you in this state?"

She touched my hand, a gesture of understanding, and though it was meant to be comforting, I couldn't help but feel shamed by my actions.

"No."

"And when they did that to you did he try and help? Make it better? Apologize?"

Another sigh. I put my forehead on the table and allowed the feelings of utter shitty-ness to wash over me. "Yes."

"So did you do right by young smitten Charlie?"

"No, but—" I sat up fast, giving myself a head rush.

"Oh, I know," she said, holding up a silencing hand. "I'm sure you had your reasons. Real, imagined, emotional *and* logical. But it's all utter bullshit. Bottom line is he didn't do anything and he wanted to right it and you used that awful, hurtful situation to put some space between you two because you were already afraid. And those childish little bitches made your worst fear come true and you took that and ran. You used it to get what you wanted, which was out."

I frowned at her. "Are you sure you manage a café? Maybe you should go into therapy, Louise."

She rolled her eyes at me and gathered her trash. "Please, this isn't therapy. This is me calling you on your bullshit. Something I've been doing, thank you very much, since we did our Coke bottle anti-smoking science project in middle school."

I snorted. "Damn it. I guess I have to call him. I'll cop to all that shit but it's still over between us."

She shook her head, her mouth a tight line of disapproval. Believe it or not, it always bothered me more when Louise disapproved of my actions than it ever had when Jack disapproved.

"What now?" I yelled.

"Why is it over?"

"Because it is!"

"Because why? Because you were having fun. Allowing yourself a little pleasure and happiness and a good old fashioned roll in the hay."

"What are you, a hundred?" I asked, laughing.

"Yes, I'm a hundred. You know what I mean."

"It's just not going to work, is all. And I know it now and he does too. Even if he doesn't want to admit it."

She held her hand up to silence me and I stared at her, uncomprehending. Finally: "What? What do you get out of this? What good is denying yourself?"

"Nothing," I mumbled but I felt my face grow red.

"Spill. We can do this the easy way or the hard way. But eventually, you'll tell me."

"He called me his girlfriend," I said. Even to my own ears it was hardly comprehensible.

"What?"

"He called me his girlfriend!" I snapped, finally getting pissed at her treating me like a child. But if I was acting like a child, how was she supposed to treat me?

"Aha!" she said, smirking. "You're *afraid*."

"No I'm not."

"Yes, you are."

"That's not it," I assured her. I repeated myself slowly so she'd hear me. "It just won't work, is all."

"Why? Let me ask you, if he were black would it not work? Or if you were Asian?"

"Of course not!"

"If he were rich and you were poor should you write it off?"

"No."

"How about if he had a Harvard education and you only had a GED. Should you just toss a chance at love?"

"No," I sighed.

"Then why does this taboo strike you so hard?"

"Because I'm not ready to be someone's girlfriend!" I yelled and then threw a French fry at her. It bounced off her forehead and we both sat there dumbstruck.

Until I started to laugh. Then we had a good old fashioned hysterical laughing fit. Something we've been doing since we were kids.

"Bitch," she said, wiping her forehead off. Then: "But seriously, Abby. What would you tell Rose to do?"

I put my head in my hands and groaned.

"What was that?"

"Tell the truth," I admitted.

"Then, Jesus, for all our sakes, just tell him the truth. Tell him you like going out with him. You like the sex. You like it all but that. That you're not ready for. Just. Tell. Him."

"Fine," I said. I reached for another fry but she slapped her hand down on mine.

"Don't even try it, sister. You get one free shot. You toss that fry and it's on."

Instead, I finally drank my wine.

CHAPTER TWELVE

I texted him Monday morning so I'd have an excuse to see him right away. I realized, once again, that he worked at the pharmacy and what a colossally stupid mistake that had been. Choosing to go out with someone who worked so damn close to me. In a place I frequented often.

On the way to work at a red light I texted Charlie with shaking fingers. WAS UNDER THE WEATHER THIS WEEKEND. WOULD LIKE TO TALK. MAYBE TONIGHT?

"Under the weather my ass," I said aloud once I hit send. "More like under the covers being a chicken."

Since my talk with Louise I'd been really angry at myself. And yet, I had no idea what to do beyond our grand plan which was to meet with him and tell him the truth.

I was still licking my divorce wounds. Twenty years of marriage, two kids and you just up and grow apart? No real rift. I mean, at one point I'd suspected an affair but it had never been confirmed. There'd been no gambling problem, sex addiction, lies, stealing or secret double life. Just— *poof* –we grew apart. Not really something that makes one eager to revisit the whole love idea.

"Not to mention he's twenty-six and he doesn't have enough life experience to really understand all this and you've only known each other a little over a week," I said. I turned into the parking lot and put the car in park. When I pulled up the emergency break I did it with a little too much gusto.

"Might be repressing some anger here," I whispered. "Just a guess. Since you just hulked out on your emergency break."

A hand hit the driver's side door and I let out a shriek, dropping my phone, clutching my chest like I was having a coronary.

Cathleen leaned down and yelled through the glass, "Who are you talking to?"

I opened the door after disengaging my seatbelt. "Well, since you just scared the shit out of me, soon I'll be talking to Jesus."

She chuckled as I rummaged on the floor for my phone. Cathleen waited while I got my work bags and locked my car.

"So what did you do this weekend? You still don't look so good. Not flushed anymore, but sort of…" She waved her hands around her face. "Draggy."

"Gee, thanks, Cat. You really know how to brighten a girl's morning."

"You know what I mean," she said, swatting my arm as if I were being silly.

"Yeah, I look old."

"Not old. Tired."

We went through the lobby, waving at Betty the receptionist.

"Well, just so you know, I spent all weekend in bed. So there you go!"

"Hmm," she said, touching her chin. "You still need something more," she said. Then she wandered off to her desk. I was hoping she'd stay there. My self-esteem couldn't take much more of Cathleen's input!

*

At ten I texted Charlie again. I'd gotten no reply to the first one. So while I waited on hold for the copier technician to give me and an ETA on his arrival, I tapped out.

DID YOU GET MY MESSAGE? MAYBE WE CAN TALK?

Then I waited. Charlie often responded with a speed that made me laugh. Like Heath and Rose he could type out ten messages in the time it took me to type one. When the tech finally got on the line and said he'd be at the office by one, I looked at the elapsed time on my phone. I'd been on hold for ten minutes and no answer from Charlie.

"He's teaching you a lesson," I whispered.

I gave it another hour. Then: LOOK, CHARLIE, I'M SORRY. I WAS JUST FREAKED OUT. CAN WE PLEASE TALK?

One o'clock came and so did the tech. His name was Ed and he was bigger than any man I'd met. When he squatted down to open up the guts of the copier he appeared as if he was still standing.

Normally, I'd have been fascinated and amused by this. But not today. Today I was getting more and more agitated by Charlie's lack of response.

He could be in a meeting, he could be asleep, he could be waiting on someone at the pharmacy, his phone could be dead. I tried to console myself over and over again that it could be a million different things. But it just *felt* as if he were giving me a taste of my own medicine.

At four o'clock, when Ed the mountain left and the copier was working, I texted Charlie a final time: FINE. I GET IT. I WAS AN ASS. I'M SORRY. REALLY. WHEN YOU WANT TO TALK—*IF* YOU WANT TO TALK—LET ME KNOW. ~A

"Let it go, let it go, walk away," I repeated to myself.

Cathleen walked by, paused when she heard my mantra and said, "You know, if you're holding onto negative things that could explain your appearance."

"You know, Cathleen," I sighed. "You are about as good for a girl's self-esteem as Carrie's "friends" at the prom," I said making finger quotes in the air.

"Who's Carrie?" she asked.

I hung my head and sighed. "Never mind," I said. Then I grabbed my stuff, turned off my laptop and hurried out of the office. I had a date with my sofa and a glass of wine. If I was lucky I could cobble together a dinner of cheese, fruit and some kind of basic sugary item.

That was the plan. However, when I found myself pulling into the parking lot of the pharmacy like some overage stalker, I can't say I was very surprised.

"This is stupid," I said to myself. "Don't do this. This isn't an eighties movie. In fact, he wasn't *born* until the eighties were almost over," I hissed.

But I found myself getting out of the car and I didn't care. My feet didn't care. My heart didn't care. I just didn't care. I'd gone from avoiding him at all costs, to needing to explain to him why I'd been such a selfish asshole.

He hadn't made me feel small and less than. His friends had. But worse than that, I had *allowed* them to make me feel that way. Because on some level I felt that way about myself way too often.

"Please be here" was the last thing I muttered as I pushed out of the growing winter gloom into the over bright interior of the pharmacy.

I saw him bent over, dark hair shielding his eyes as he stocked a shelf. He raised his head, turning, "Hi there, welcome to Franklin pharm—"

His eyes met mine and something in my stomach twisted with electricity and my mouth went dry. First his eyes lit up and so did his face. Then a look of gloom quickly shuttered his initial reaction.

"Hi, Abby," he said.

"You didn't answer me," I blurted.

"Terrible when someone won't answer you, isn't it?" he asked, turning back to continue stacking chewy sweet and sour candies on the shelf.

"I'm sorry!" More blurting.

He said nothing. But I saw him pause in his repetitive motion.

"I'm..." I inhaled and then tried to calm my racing thoughts. "I'm going home and get something to eat. I don't know what time you get off—"

"Six," he said, still not looking up.

Less than an hour. That electric thing in my gut seemed to wiggle its way up into my heart.

"Well, if you want to have a glass of wine or a beer or just a cup of tea and...talk, I'll be at home. I'd like to explain, Charlie. But it's really up to you now."

He nodded once. Not telling me if I'd see him or not. His jaw was set, his face turned away. I could tell he was angry but the overriding emotion I picked up on from Charlie was hurt.

He was hurt. And I had been the one to hurt him. Which completely sucked, I was now starting to realize.

"I'll be home," I said again, softly, as an elderly lady pushed a cart full of tissues and hand sanitizer to the front counter.

Then I fled the pharmacy and its brightness on wobbly legs. I hoped he'd come. I truly did. It didn't escape me how truly bipolar my emotions had been over the last few days. Hopefully I could chalk it up to getting my feet wet again in the dating pool. And not the fact that I'd reacted like a spoiled kid. Punishing Charlie for something he hadn't done.

*

I found myself unable to eat or drink. I sat and stared at a rerun of a sitcom that had been popular around the time my kids had been born. When the doorbell rang I'd given up hope on him, so it took me by surprise.

My hands were shaking and I rubbed them against my leggings. "Easy, girl."

When I opened the door Charlie stood there, wind blowing his dark hair, his cheeks red from the cold. "Hi," he said.

"Hi," I said. "Want to come in?"

"No."

My heart dropped. "Charlie—"

The wind blew and I heard it howl lightly as if we were in a bad horror movie. Charlie rustled inside his inadequate coat. "On second thought…" He stepped inside and shut the door. "I'm angry but not stupid. It's too fucking cold to prove a point by standing out there."

I touched his frigid lapels and then, judging by his face,

surprised us both by touching his cheek. "I'm sorry I was such an ass," I said.

He took my hand and pulled it back. "I'm sorry you were such an ass too."

That took me by surprise and I stared at him. Those bright blue eyes, looking a bit shaded beneath like he hadn't been sleeping quite enough lately. And the dark stubble starting to sprout on his chin. And the full pout of his mouth...slightly twisted into a half grin.

A slow trickle of laughter started to flow and then I found myself laughing. In earnest. The hardest I had laughed since I'd seen him last. And the best part was Charlie was laughing with me. Not quite as hard as I was. Not quite as insane-person as me. But he was laughing. And I held myself up by leaning on him.

I looked up in his face. "You scared me," I said, laying it all out. "When you called me your girlfriend. You scared the hell out of me," I said between trickling aftershocks of laughter. "And I used what your jerky friends did as an excuse to put distance between us. Instead of telling you the truth."

His expression had gone from wary amusement to kind concern. It sparked a tiny flame of peace within me to see him looking at me like that. He wasn't going to hold this against me forever.

"I'm sorry," I said. "Charlie, I'm so sorry. For real. That was unfair of me and I wouldn't blame you if you didn't forgive me but—"

He snagged my wrists and tugged me to him, cutting off the end of the sentence by kissing me. I realized as his lips crushed against mine and I felt the first gentle stroke of his tongue that I had truly missed that kiss over the past few days.

That knowledge was terrifying if I allowed myself to ponder it for any amount of time.

So I didn't.

I wrapped my arms around his neck and kissed him back. Parting my lips, meeting the touch of his tongue with my own. When his hands settled on my hips, I closed that final distance between us and pressed my body against his.

He was hard. He was cold. And he was eager because he immediately wrapped his arm around my waist to secure me close.

"I missed you, Ace. I missed kissing you. Touching you." As he said the words, he pushed his hands up beneath my tunic. When he found me braless he groaned, pushing his lower body against me more firmly.

"Me too, me too, me too," I kept saying like an idiot. I still felt this would never work. I still felt it was doomed. But I *wanted* this part to work. I wanted us to recognize this for what it was and then it would be okay.

No strings. No expectations. My fuzzy romantic notions. Sex. Company. A fling. That's all this could be.

Before I could say those words, before I could say anything at all, he bent his knees, caught me around the thighs, picked me up and took me to the bedroom.

"I hope this is okay," he muttered just before he dropped me to the bed.

"Yes," I said. "Yes, yes." Another mindless mantra of pleasure inspired by Charlie.

CHAPTER THIRTEEN

He pulled my tunic off before he even took off his coat. Covered me with himself, the thin wool lapels draping me like wings. Charlie's teeth scraped softly along my throat, over my earlobe. He sucked my nipple into his mouth, bit until I hissed, soothed it with soft licks until I squirmed. So wet between the legs I was mindless but for my arousal.

"I hope you don't mind if I don't take my time. And if I'm not a gentleman," he said, pushing my leggings down. I was bare beneath those too. I always got comfortable the instant I got home from work. Always. I'd never been so grateful for the routine. Charlie growled softly, shucked his coat and pinned my thighs to the bed. I was spread wide, bared to him and he covered my pussy with his mouth, found my thumping clit with his tongue. He sucked and licked until I was thrusting up from beneath him, completely oblivious to anything but the feel of his mouth on me.

When I came, I shut my eyes, clutching the bed sheets and simply said, "I don't mind" in way of answering his question. A second spasm hit me just as he thrust his fingers deep inside me and I said "Charlie!" as pleasure washed over me.

He stood, stripping down until he was bare. I studied him for the few heartbeats he stood there watching me. Lean, strong legs, flat belly, hard cock standing out straight and ready. His chest was firm but not too buff, same with his arms. I smiled at him and he smiled back. Him there, naked, ready, wanting me was the best thing I'd see in ages. And I'd allowed myself that moment to really see his arousal. His attraction. I'd allowed myself the luxury and I was so glad.

"Charlie," I said again and the smile went away. His eyes darkened with lust. He covered me with his body again, knocking my legs wide, pushing his lean hips between my thighs and entered me on a single hard stroke. It stole my breath and his because we inhaled in unison as if we were about to dive underwater.

"Jesus," he sighed, moving in me with a firm, desperate rhythm from the get-go.

I wrapped my legs around his waist, opening to him more. I arched up to take him as deep as I could, mashing my breasts to his warm chest. I shut my eyes, soaking in the sensation of his hands touching me everywhere and anywhere he could. His fingers stroked my hair before traveling gently along my shoulders, down my sides. When he laid a hand over my throat and kissed me, the heavy sensation of his hand there, his mouth covering mine, his cock filling me was all too much. I felt overwhelmed and at his mercy right then and I came with a shocking shiver that seemed to bolt through me like a jolt of electricity.

"There's my girl," he said, rocking his hips from side to side. The words *my girl* and the fear they evoked, mixed with the suddenness of the orgasm and the fact that his big hand was still on my neck, covering my pulse, caused it to happen again. A short, softer orgasm that was no less surprising than the first.

He shook his head, gritting his teeth. "Yeah, I survived one, Abby, but two is too much." His hips moved faster and his eyes were heavy lidded. "To know I did that. Caused that. That I bring you pleasure—" he cut off his own words by kissing me. I moved up beneath him, wanting his pleasure to be even a fraction as good as mine had been.

When he came he went rigid in my arms and then sighed heartily. The orgasm shook him and I wrapped my arms around him to hold him close. I surprised myself when I said "Stay the night, Charlie."

*

It was dark in the room. Very dark because it was well past midnight. I could hear Charlie's deep breathing but I was wide awake. Still examining why I had spontaneously invited him to stay and what it meant way deep down. What it meant fairly close to the surface was that I trusted Charlie. No matter how many protestations I tossed out into the universe. No matter how much I fought myself and Louise and anyone else who tried to weigh in, I trusted Charlie.

Because bottom line, Charlie was trustworthy.

In his sleep, he rolled to his side and threw an arm across my belly. A warm sense of satisfaction invaded me and I fought it. I would not get used to this. Trust or no trust. I sighed at my own mental battle with myself and he whispered to me. Not asleep after all.

"You liked that a lot."

I jumped when he spoke and laughed nervously to cover it. "I thought you were asleep."

His fingers trailed back and forth across my stomach, it almost tickled but not quite. "Nope."

"Oh."

"You didn't answer me," he said.

"Liked what?" I was confused. "The sex?"

He leaned over me, propped up on one elbow. I couldn't see anything beyond the shadowed outline of Charlie. But I could tell by his posture that he was looking down at me. "Yes, that, but…" he chuckled in the dark. "You always like that. *I* always like that. What's not to like?"

I joined his laughter but found I was holding my breath, waiting for him to explain. His hand slid up to trace the full outline of my breasts, he found my nipples and circled them too but kept moving. His hands slipped along my collar bone and then swept across my shoulders. And finally it settled, a heavy presence, on my throat.

"This," he said. And then he very gently put a touch more pressure so I could truly feel the weight of his hand.

"Oh that." I tried to brush it off. Even as I spoke and found my voice only barely impeded by his hand, I grew wetter between my legs. When Charlie's in the vicinity I'm almost always aroused on some level, but this had me drenched. Ready for him. On the verge of begging him to take me. Just to let me have that release.

"Did you know that before?" he asked. He kept his hand on my throat and kissed me.

The kiss pulled a small groan out of me. I was so worked up just from the timbre of his voice and the feel of his fingers pressed there against my vulnerable flesh, that the kiss was the final straw. It was impossible to hide how turned-on I was when I made noises like that.

"Answer me, Ace." He removed his hand and I felt the absence of the extra weight. Those fingers appeared elsewhere when he slipped his hand between my legs and nudged my nether lips. He briefly pressed against my clit and I made another desperate sound. Then his fingers slipped inside me as easy as you please. He thrust deep, stimulating all the hidden nerve endings deep inside that were primed for any pleasure he delivered.

When he returned his hand to my throat I could smell myself on him. I could also feel the primitive sound of blood in my pussy, my temples, and my throat.

"Yeah, I've known."

"So…" He moved slowly, in the dark, to straddle my hips. His cock pressed hard against my lower belly. His hand never moved. He leaned in and kissed me softly. I whimpered. "Were you not telling me because I'm new or—"

Before he could finish the sentence I began shaking my head. I wasn't able to shake it much given his grip on me but enough to get my point across. "No, no," I said. "I never would have told anyone."

"Why?" Another kiss. Then he moved slowly from side to side on my hips so I could feel his erection taunting me.

"Because I told Jack once. It happened by accident. His hand there. And the same reaction…from me, I mean," I stammered. "And he said…" I shook my head again, unwilling to continue.

He moved his hand and I swallowed a small cry. I refused to admit what it did for me, his hand there. Charlie spread out over me, pressed his whole body along mine so we were thigh to thigh, hip to hip, belly to belly. He brushed my hair back out of my face as I fought myself not to ask him to return his hand to my neck and then fuck me.

"He said what, Ace?"

"Charlie—"

Hi kissed me quiet and then said, "Tell me. Please I promise you, you can. I promise you I'll understand. And I won't say anything to make you feel bad."

Boy had he nailed that.

My breath shuddered in my lungs and I finally pushed myself to say it. I did trust Charlie. He'd never given me any reason not to.

I moved my hips up, showing him I wanted him, and part of me trying to distract him. "He said it was strange. And that I shouldn't say that. It was the equivalent of asking to be hurt. And who the hell wanted to be hurt."

I said it all in an impossibly soft voice because the way Jack had made me feel when I'd told him that I'd like the feel of his hand on my neck while he fucked me was simple: he'd made me feel shame.

"Well, that's very judgmental of him," Charlie said and put his hand back. My pulse pounded beneath his grip and ratcheted up from the pressure.

"I—"

"Shh, just let me make you come, okay? And I'll keep my hand here where you like it. Where it gets you off. Because it's fine. If it's good for you and hurts no one, then it's good. You're not hurting anyone, are you, Abby?" He parted my thighs by wriggling his hips.

"No," I sighed. I was so wet between the legs. My body ached for him. I'd never understood that saying, but now I did. My body demanded him, craved him, drummed out the sound of the world with blood because it wanted him so badly. When he entered me it was like inhaling after holding your breath for a very long time.

"I agree." He thrust into me deep, not talking any more. His hand over my throat was a third party to our fucking.

I struggled to hold on even as I very mildly had to struggle for air. He knew exactly how to read me, using the perfect pressure for me to feel his hand there but not actually cutting off my respiration or hurting me. There would be no marks on my neck, just marks on my soul. I'd remember, probably until I was old and gray, how Charlie had understood me and given me what I craved.

His thrust grew harsher and he whispered in my ear, "You're so damn tight, Abby. You feel so good. I missed you. Missed this. Thank you for telling me." When he said it and squeezed very lightly with that hand, I came. Sobbing in the dark, overcome with emotion I hadn't expected. But it felt good. Like I had been scrubbed clean from the inside out.

He shushed me, kissed my leaking eyes and said, "Ace, you get me every time." Then he came, shuddering over me, his hand finally leaving my throat.

When my alarm went off at 7:30, I woke pleasantly sore. When I thought of what we'd done, his hand there, excitement leapt in my blood. The memories of the night before settled beautifully heavy on me.

"Work, Abby," I said, hurrying out of bed. I'd definitely need a shower. And where was Charlie?

Instead of him, I found a note stuck to the coffee machine. "It's ready to go for you. I had the first shift at work. Had to go. Didn't want to wake you. Thank you for telling me. Love, Charlie."

I realized I missed him. I wasn't really sure how I felt about that. So I forced myself to focus on the fact that I was borderline late and took that shower I needed so badly.

CHAPTER FOURTEEN

It took my entire lunch break to explain it all to Louise. I had to go out and sit in my car despite the temperatures because one cannot give full details of sex like I'd had in the middle of a room full of people. Not even if you whisper.

"So you're not breaking up with him?"

"No. I guess not. I think at some point I need to do the whole parameters of our relationship thing."

"You told him you're not ready to be anyone's girlfriend."

"Yeah, that's about it, but then all the sex happened."

She snorted. "Yeah, it just magically happened. You had nothing to do with that sex part, did you?"

"I...shut up!" I said, but she had me laughing.

"Oh, I'm giving you a heads up and then I have to run, Michelle's big fiftieth birthday party is coming up. Beginning of March. You'll be getting an invite but it's a swanky party and you need to bring someone."

"Why?"

"Well," she said. "You don't *have* to bring someone. But I'm bringing someone. And so are most of the girls we hang with. Must be a good year for the singles in our group. Even Denise found a guy at the post office of all places. He's a mail carrier!"

This seemed to tickle Louise to no end.

"Who are you bringing?" I asked.

"Keith." She sounded just a tiny bit defiant.

"He's back!" I said.

"Yes. And he ate a ton of crow."

"He told you that you were too fat," I said, feeling a spark of anger. Louise is lovely, lush, curvy, and a pleasure to hug. She is not fat.

"He's an ass. What can I say? But somehow all this *fat* he made a comment on was exactly what he missed cuddling. And let's not forget fucking. I am a terror in the sack."

I giggled, unable to cover my mouth in time. "TMI!" I shouted.

"No such thing between the likes of us. Now I do have to go. We have a new waitress and she looks like she's ready to go full mutiny on this here eating establishment. Love you, sweetie. Don't forget about that party. Or that you need a *date*."

I hit end on my phone and sighed. "Oh you are just loving this."

For some reason my best friend's favorite pastime was torturing me.

I texted Charlie asking if he wanted to meet for food tonight. Meet. Out. In public. Let's see how another outing went. If we could go out in public without any pitchforks or torches or angry villagers.

My phone jingled. MILLIGAN'S AT 8?

PERFECT.

I went back to work and tried to concentrate on my input

in the employee reviews. My boss kept looking at me. I had a feeling she knew that part of my brain was out in left field. But more accurately, it wasn't out in left field, it was in Charlie's pants.

*

"So are we okay?" Charlie bit into a sandwich roughly the size of my head, while I chased a Santa Fe eggroll around my plate with a fork before giving up and grabbing it with my fingers.

"Us? Yeah, fine," I stammered. "Why?"

"Well, we kind of skimmed the issue last night but then…" He shook his head and grinned at me. That grin went right to the center of me, making my blood pound in my veins.

"The sex happened," I snorted.

"Exactly. Were we done talking or was that it?. I used the "G-word"."

"Girlfriend," I sighed, nibbling the crispiest bits along the outside of my eggroll.

"Yes, that."

"Don't call me that," I said matter-of-factly. "I'm not ready."

His eyes showed his amusement. There they were again—endearing to me—the very faint beginnings of very fine lines at the edges of his eyes. It made him more handsome. "Okay, duly noted."

"Right. Good. I just…" I shrugged. "I was with Jack for so damn long. Then when we split, it just gutted me. I had days when I didn't think I'd survive." I shook my head, my appetite gone. I put my napkin on the edge of the table, sipped my drink. "I know that sounds really fucking melodramatic, but when you have an idea of how your life is going to go for oh…half your life, and it all blows up in your face, it's terrifying."

"I can imagine."

I held up my fingers. "It was all mapped out. Marriage, kids, kids off to school, empty nest, time alone, honeymoon revisited, travel, grandchildren, grandparenthood." I laughed but something in my chest ached.

"And then—"

"And then before the empty nest part, things started to turn to shit and we grew apart and very quickly, mind you, he found a…" I stumbled on the next part. "A woman and then all the sudden the house is divided, the kids are reeling. Hell, I was reeling. And so was he. Neither of us expected that game plan to take a severe left turn. Neither of us anticipated a detour from that well thought out roadmap to our lives."

"But there it was," he said, covering my hand with his.

"There it was." I swallowed hard "So after getting myself out of the funk of my marriage taking a header into the crapper," I snorted, "Not to put too fine a point on it."

He squeezed my hand, laughed. His beer and his sandwich sat there neglected. All Charlie's focus was on me. It was one of the things I loved most about him.

The thought hit me like a rock to the head and I blinked away tears and pushed it away. It was just a figure of speech.

"But now," he said, squeezing again. "You have this big blank page to write on. So to speak."

"A blank page is scarier at forty-two than at twenty-something," I said, softly.

"Maybe, but it's still about how you look at it." He took a bite of his dinner and chewed thoughtfully. I watched him. Feeling like Charlie, the kid I wrote off for being so young way too often, was about to teach me something.

"You know, I just read an article while I was shelving magazines at the pharmacy." He winked at me and I laughed. "It said that your body doesn't know the difference between stress and excitement." He shrugged. "Your body releases the same hormones when you're stressed as they do when you're excited."

I watched him, waiting for the point.

"And?"

"And...the only part of you that knows the difference is your brain." He reached across and tapped my temple very softly with his fingertip.

"So..."

"So tell your brain you're excited," he said. "That it's an adventure. Your body is all messed up half the time anyway, but if your brain thinks this is all exciting shit, then you're golden." He shrugged and the nonchalant act made me wanted to climb across the table and plant myself in his lap. "Besides, you have to admit. I'm pretty exciting."

I snorted, and began to pick at my eggroll again. "You think so, hunh?"

"I do. And if you take me home I'll prove it."

Excitement waterfalled inside me. Seeming to start at the top of my head before rippling down to my toes. "I think I'll take you up on that," I said. "But first I need to ask you something, exciting not-boyfriend person."

"What's that?"

"Well, there's this big party coming up..."

*

"I told you I'd prove it," Charlie said, two hours later. He rested his chin on my hipbone, his hands smoothing up and down my thigh as he watched me.

My body still let off small spasms and echoes of my pleasure. I laughed, "You did."

"I guess I'll—"

"Stay," I said.

He looked unsure for the first time. Something in his gaze made me wary.

"I'm okay for you as long as I don't put a name to this, is that it?"

"Right now," I said. My mouth felt suddenly dry. Was he angry?

He nodded, his chin pushing against my hip hard enough to sting, hard enough to get me aroused all over again. He caught the look and parted my nether lips with his fingers. Slid two inside me. I arched up to take them.

"Are you okay with that?" I said, my voice breathy from want.

"For now," he said. "But what happens when that changes, Ace?"

"We re-evaluate," I said.

We didn't have to re-evaluate for ages. Or it felt like ages. A few weeks, at least. Not until Michelle's party. That was the night of reckoning. And the time went fast. You know what they say, time flies when you're having fun. Or tons of sex.

CHAPTER FIFTEEN

"Jack, I have to get going soon." I looked at the clock nervously. The party was in four hours. I had a lot to do. I had to do my hair, press my dress, spackle my face. I snorted.

"What's so funny about this? You're dating some kid, not much older than ours!"

He'd come to see Heath and Rose who had magically gotten a chance to come the night before and spend the night. Her from college, him from base. I'd invited their father to stop in and see them as a courtesy. But it seemed the divorced exes grapevine had done its job and he'd come over primed to fight about Charlie.

"I was laughing because I have a looooot to do and none of it involves arguing with you."

He frowned at me. I knew that frown. It was the patriarchal think-about-this-you-are-wrong-I-am-right frown. I hated that frown. As much as I had once loved the man standing before me, I hated that face he pulled.

"Abby."

"Dad, if I'm not mistaken, Rita is younger than Charlie."

Rita was Jack's current girlfriend and about two years younger than Charlie. I grinned but said nothing. I'd let my daughter handle this.

"Rose, now is not the time to pull your—"

"Her what? Her opinion?" I intervened. "The kids and I talked last night and they're fine with this. He's twenty-six, not seventeen, Jack. I have sixteen years on him. Let's see, you're forty-five and Rita's twenty-four. My math says—"

"Twenty-one," Rose said and then giggled.

"Math was never your strong suit, mom," Heath said and then chuckled.

Jack looked fit to be tied. "This is not about me or about Rita or about anything but you, Abby."

"What? Me moving on with my life? Me having a guy in my life? A nice guy. Who's way more than just his age?"

"Abby—"

"Uh oh, the warning voice," I sighed.

He sputtered.

I put a hand on his chest and began to steer him toward the door. "Look Jack, I talked long into the night over pizza and ice cream with our children about me and Charlie. And they are fine with it. I hate to break the news to you, but right now, at this point in my life, *their* opinions matter to me. Yours…not so much. We're divorced. Which means you have no opinion."

Heath came up and clapped his father on the shoulder. "Come on dad. Walk us to the car. I have to get Rose back to school before I make a few stops. Have to get back to base tomorrow night. And you know if I'm not there to check in on time it's my ass. Time is money, like you always said."

Jack tossed me another glare and I saw his reaction for what it was. Jealousy. It was fine for him to parade a few babes around after our divorce. Not so okay for me to find someone young and handsome and exciting to spend my time with.

It was almost amusing except it was a little sad too.

We'd built a life together once. Brought kids into the world. Made plans. And now we were practically strangers and half the time he was angry with me for living my life. I didn't get it. And I didn't have time to ponder it.

I hurried out, swiftly kissed my kids one more time, whispered "thanks" in Rose's ear and watched her dissolve into more laughter.

"He'll be okay," she whispered back. "He's just confused."

"About what?"

"You having a life."

I rolled my eyes and watched them go. I was just about to go inside to find my iron when Rose came running back. "You know mom, Heath and I were talking last night and if this guy really means something to you…"

"Yeah?" My face had gone a little numb. Her words made me nervous.

"You're going to have to let us meet him."

I groaned. "I know. But first let me get through my first big event with him. If I survive that, I'll consider it."

She gave me a peck on the cheek, "Good mother," she said and then patted my head.

I hurried inside and focused on the next hurdle. A gaggle of forty-somethings fueled by a shit-ton of liquor. But Rose's words kept echoing in my mind. *If this guy really means something to you…*

"He's just a fling," I said to myself in the mirror. But I wasn't so sure I was telling the truth anymore.

*

"You're going to break my arm," he whispered.

I stopped in my tracks despite the cold March wind that was pressing my dress to my legs and invading my hosiery. "I'm sorry. I'm sorry. I'm a little nervous."

"I'm not *that* ugly," Charlie said.

"You're not ugly at all!" I said. "You're just new. To all of them. My god, you'll be on display. I have flashbacks of the party you took me to. Then I fear that my friends will be harder on you than yours were on me."

"Those girls who were so rude to you aren't really friends. They're the girlfriends of my friends. They're acquaintances." He had pressed his pretty full lips together in dissatisfaction.

Without thinking, I took his face n my hands, his dark hair just a shade longer than when I met him, curled over my fingers. I kissed him. A real kiss. Not a peck. And honest to god we're-in-this-together kiss. It felt so good.

"Careful or I'm going to toss you back in that car and fuck you until you sob."

I dropped my head to his chest. "Don't tempt me. That sounds better than the party."

Charlie slipped his arm through mine. "Oh, come on, Ace. This is great. I can meet your friends. Hey," he jostled me playfully. "You can show me off."

I was just about to ask him if he was stuck up much when he stopped in his tracks beneath a streetlight. "Oh, I almost forgot," he said.

He reached in his pocket and pulled out a small blue velveteen box. My heart stumbled over itself and I had to force myself to draw a shivery breath. "Charlie—"

"Don't panic," he chuckled. "It's not an engagement ring.

But it's something I saw down in one of the shops of Ellicott City that reminded me of you."

"Of me?"

"Yes! I just said that!" he teased. He kissed me. It went straight to my toes and then curled up, that warm attraction.

I opened the box as he held it steady. "Oh…" I said. "Oh wow."

I'd never have bought it for myself, but seeing it, my face split into a smile at the fact that it was mine. A very tiny playing card suspended from a silver chain. It was rimmed in silver itself, and it was the Ace of Spades. The spade itself seemed to be drifting off on one corner. When I squinted at it beneath the bright sodium lights, I saw it seemed to be composed of smoke. It was magical, the teeny tiny playing card.

"Do you like it?"

"I love it."

"An ace for my Ace," he said, putting it around my neck. The card nestled in my cleavage. He pushed his hands gently into my hair and kissed me. "Now let's go in." Charlie pulled me along. We were nearing the entrance, then he said, conversationally, "Do you know what the spade is said to represent?"

"No. What?"

There was that grin again. It only made the fact that he'd come clean shaven and prettied up just for me more obvious. He was always pretty. In fact, I found him even prettier with the stubble on his face and his hair all artfully mussed. But he'd done this for me and it made me feel like I'd been struck by a tiny bolt of lightning.

His hand slid down on my ass as we stood there behind another couple waiting to enter. I felt myself gasp more than heard it. He squeezed gently and the feel of him gripping my bottom went right to my pussy. "A woman's ass. I've always thought, a woman's *spankable* ass," he whispered as the line moved forward.

I had to dig in my bag for our invitation and after what he said my vision was blurred and my ears were ringing. It didn't help that my hands were shaking and I could feel the somehow cool yet warm presence of that ace of spades on my throat. I wondered if there was a coat closet or an alcove or a nook where we could sneak off and fuck like rabbits. My cheeks had just blossomed with guilty heat when I heard Louise's voice. "There she is. And who is *this*?"

Please be nice to him, please be nice to him... The mantra rushed through my head as I handed the greeter our invitation and he instructed me that we were at table nine.

"I'm at nine too!" Louise said, taking Charlie's arm and leading him off. "Lucky us."

I gritted my teeth but Charlie seemed charmed. "Hi there," he said.

"Hi there back at you, Charlie. I'm Louise. I'm her best friend. I'm shocked—" she cut herself off to look over her shoulder to throw me a shaming glance. "—that we haven't met yet. But we will rectify that tonight. And lucky for us, there's plenty of booze!"

I realized I was holding my breath when my vision got fuzzy around the edges. I fingered the necklace and smiled. I'd breathe and be calm and breathe some more. It would be fine.

And it was all fine. He met Louise, who proceeded to almost entirely ignore her date and tell Charlie every embarrassing thing I'd ever done. Including my toilet paper tail at her father's funeral. We ate, we drank, and we were merry.

We wished Michelle a beautiful birthday and she fawned over pretty, pretty Charlie and how kind he was.

Everything was fine.

Until after Michelle left and the party started to wind down. For the first time since his hand had been on my ass, he pulled me in and touched me intimately. His hand snaking down to cup my right cheek as we made our way to the door. And that was when Gabby Stover—the only woman at the party I couldn't stand—opened her big, opinionated mouth.

"Can you believe this happy horse shit? What's he, ten?"

Whoever was with her snorted. But it was a noncommittal snort and I couldn't tell anything beyond the fact that it was an acknowledging sound.

I froze and Charlie felt it. He'd heard her. Everyone within her vicinity had. "Keep walking, Ace." He said it out the side of his mouth. His warm breath brushed my ear and his hand moved up to tighten on my waist.

Normally, his reassurance and support would have been enough to keep me going. But then I heard:

"Is he holding onto her so he won't get lost? Where's his teacher? Aren't all kids supposed to be accounted for before they board the bus?" She laughed; it was an ugly sound. My heart broke for Charlie because I'd been exactly where he was at that fateful house party.

The person with Gabby said, "Gabby...hush."

That made me take a deep breath. She was alone in her cruelty. She was out there lost in nasty-girl land.

I turned fast even though Charlie tried to steady me and Louise reached out to put a hand on my arm.

"Shut it, Gabby," I said. Boy, that felt impotent.

Louise's fingers tightened on my arm. "Stupidity is fueled by wine," she said. Reminding me that the three of us had polished off three bottles of a wonderful Cabernet.

I had plenty of fuel.

But it had been such a lovely night. My best friend, my new…Charlie. We'd all been talking and getting along and laughing and now this. My own personal forty-something version of the mean girls at the house party. My own personal jerk here to make Charlie feel bad for something as inconsequential as his age.

"Oh, wow. Did it take you long to think that up?" She snickered. Her friend shook her head and broke away, going out the side door.

"Gabby, leave it alone," Louise said. "Don't you have a broom waiting to take you home somewhere?"

"Come on, Abby," Charlie said, pulling me gently.

But I didn't want to budge.

"Is this how you get over a marriage that failed? You date a first grader?"

It wasn't so much the dig at my marriage failing. I'd had a failed marriage, so had Louise and if gossip served, so had Gabby. It was the dig at Charlie. Charlie who had done nothing wrong and, if anything, had miraculously managed to teach me a few things about myself over the last few weeks.

I pulled my arm free of him and felt him give another desperate grab, but I was moving. Despite hearing Louise chanting, "Abby—Abby…Abby!"

I found myself toe to toe with Gabby. Short, dumpy Gabby to my tall, curvy brunette self. She'd been a bitch in high school and apparently, she still was.

"Take it back," I hissed. In the back of my mind, the sober part, I knew how trivial and stupid and cliché that sounded. And yet, with some wine under my invisible belt and Charlie there to protect, for that's what I felt I was doing, it seemed too fucking important.

"I will not. You cow."

"Cow?"

She nodded. I could see how alcohol-shiny her eyes were. And I had no doubt that mine were probably well on their way, if not, already, equally shiny. But…cow?"

I inched forward, practically on top of her. "Take. It. Back."

"I. Will. Not." She grinned and I saw she was still as evil as could be even twenty-some-odd years later. "Isn't he about due for a nap? A diaper cha—"

I didn't really notice I was moving until I had ahold of her hair and her head reared back. "Take it back!" I bellowed as if I were trapped in some 80s barbarian movie.

It was quite horrifying, being aware of it way back in the non-crazy part of my head.

"Let me go, you bitch. Your boyfriend needs his binky."

I let her go, alright. And when Gabby took a sloppy swing at me, I dodged it and then clocked her. My knuckles glancing off her cheekbone. My wrist bent uncomfortably forward but I definitely decked her because she went down, legs splayed.

"Jesus!" Louise said, rushing forward.

But I wasn't done. And neither was that witch. She had ahold of my ankle and was desperately trying to yank me to the ground.

She got me good and I dropped like a stone. "You…*cunt*," I hissed.

We all froze then. Me, Louise, Charlie. Even Gabby. I'd never used that word in my life but it was the first thing that came to mind. Probably because I'd never used it and it seemed so taboo.

Gabby's eyes went wide and she let out a shriek. She grabbed my long hair and snapped my head back. I didn't think, I swept my leg to the side and basically punted her a foot across the slick, freshly waxed floor.

Unfortunately my hair went with her because she kept it clasped in her grubby little fist. I heard a horrific noise, it brought to mind a pterodactyl. As I moved toward her, slackening her grip on my hair by my proximity, I realized the sound was me. I hit her full force, pushing her back on the floor. She released my hair and I smacked her face. Not hard enough to leave a mark but hard enough to make a sound. She squawked again and tried to hit me but I managed to straddle her so that my legs locked her arms to her side. She waved them wildly despite them being pinned and the overall image of her under me was of one of those gray-brown potato bugs we used to poke when we were kids just to see them curl up.

"Take it back," I hissed.

"You're insane."

"I have to agree," Louise said softly. I shot her a glare.

"You were evil in school and you're evil now. You're jealous and horrible and you deserved to get decked a long time ago."

"You're nuts," she said.

"Hey," I shrugged. "You hit me. I was simply defending myself."

I heard Charlie laugh softly at that. Then to Louise: "It's true."

The event people were headed our way and I knew I had to get up. But if I got up she'd try something, I knew it.

"Get up, get up," Louise growled softly.

"You're a petty, ignorant, *evil* woman," I said, though I'd already used evil. My brain cells were soaked in wine, evil was the best I was going to conjure.

"Let me up."

Charlie put out his hand and I took it with as much dignity as I could muster. "He's a man. A good man. A...a...man's man," I said triumphantly as if I had just proven something.

I heard Louise and Charlie snicker. God damn it, they were supposed to be backing me up.

"Whatever," Gabby said.

"Oh, not so much to say now that someone's taken you down a notch," I said, stumbling only a bit as Charlie righted me. Louise rushed forward to smooth my dress down. Static cling had it sticking to me like a ruched drapery.

"Take your toddler boyfriend home, Abby," she said.

There was that pterodactyl noise again. I lunged and heard Charlie whisper, "Okay, okay, Mike Tyson. We're done for the night." And then the world was turning because he was turning me and then we were outside and it was cold and clear and lovely.

I turned to Charlie and Louise. "Feels nice out here," I said smiling. "Very crisp. I was getting a little hot."

Louise rolled her eyes.

"Let's get you home, slugger," Charlie said. "You're looking a little..."

"Green," Louise filled in.

Turns out I was green. Very green. When we got home, I proved it. Instead of a night to remember in bed, Charlie stayed with me for a night to remember in the bathroom.

I turned to him near dawn and said, "I still say it was the fist fight. I assure you, I can drink. But that was my first bar brawl."

He snorted. "In the shower, Ace."

Then he put me to bed, crawled in after me and we fell asleep just as the sun came up.

I dreamed about a single word in giant white letters. The B was twice as tall as I was. The O looked like a tunnel to the unknown.

He'd just spent hours tending to me as I proceeded to show him my worst. So is it really a surprise that I dreamt of the word BOYFRIEND until noon when we woke up?

CHAPTER SIXTEEN

I woke to him kissing my knuckles. The kisses moved to my shoulder. I shivered, smiled. "You'll have to let me get up and brush my teeth," I whispered. When I felt how dry my mouth was, I added, "And drink a bucket of water."

He laughed, patted my ass beneath the covers. "Go on, then. Go and brush and drink. Because when you get back, all bets are off."

I sat up and pushed my toes into the deep, chocolate brown carpeting. It was one of the small luxuries of my new apartment. The landlord had taken his deceased parents' home and renovated it into two apartments. Lucky for me, in the process, he'd spared no expense. He wanted good tenants willing to pay a good price and he'd made sure to make the place enticing.

I squished my toes into the shag once more.

"You are running out of time. I'm about to pounce whether you brush those teeth or not." He made a faux swipe for me and I shot to my feet squealing.

"I'm going! I'm going!" I said, running from the

bedroom. The apartment was cold and my small pink nightgown wasn't much of a barrier. I hurried into the bathroom, peed, and then brushed my teeth.

In the mirror my reflection regarded me. Brown hair all mussed with bed head, but fairly sexy, I thought, turning my head this way and that. My cheeks were kissed with the blush that always comes from excitement and arousal. My chest above my breasts flushed. A fairly amazing appearance considering the night I'd put in.

He made me feel alive, I realized. I felt more me when I was with Charlie. More willing to stomp my foot and say 'this is who I am'. He didn't change me, he augmented me. He didn't dictate my behavior, he stood by it.

"He is a good man," I said after spitting out toothpaste. Those were the words I'd said to Gabby the night before and now I said them to myself.

I hurried into the kitchen and drank a tumbler of filtered water. It almost slaked my thirst. Getting drunk was for kids, I thought. I was not a kid anymore.

"I'm coming to get you if you don't hurry!" he called and I laughed. But I realized he was fine. So he was the kid. He was the young one. The one who could still go out and party and be fine when the sun came up.

My heart plummeted. One moment I was invigorated, the next I was disheartened. I was torn, I realized. Was he a man or was he a kid? How did I really feel?

I sighed.

"Ace!"

"I'm coming," I said, pushing it all away. Simply focusing on the fact that my blood was up and my nipples were tight and my body was already craving him. Having him in me.

I hit the bed with a thud, bounced and only stopped when

he grabbed my waist and held onto me. Kissing me.

"There she is. Hopefully, fully brushed and full of water." Charlie flipped me and pinned me. My dark hair strewn across my eyes obstructing my view a little bit. It was definitely a turn on.

"I'm full of water, freshly brushed."

"I went for the old Altoid routine. I've barely slept anyway."

"Why?" I asked, concern overriding my arousal a little. "Are you okay?"

Charlie distracted me by dropping soft kisses along the worn lace that outlined the bodice of my nightgown. My skin blossomed with goose bumps where his mouth touched me. I moved beneath him, both wanting him to confess to me and to say nothing and keep going.

"I was just wondering some things..." He pulled my bodice down and sucked my nipple hard enough for my pussy to flex greedily. God, how I wanted him in me.

"What things? What things?" I panted.

"Did you get upset with that woman because she called me a toddler?" he asked, pushing my nightgown high and then pulling me up a bit so we could maneuver it off. Before I could answer, he went on, "Or because she called me your boyfriend? And by upset I mean did you hit her because of what she called me?" He laughed softly, his lips skimming my hip and caressing the place low on my belly just above my mound.

"Charlie—"

"Shh," he said, parting my legs, pushing a finger inside me so I rippled around him wetly. "You don't have to answer me now. In fact, why don't you ponder that and tell me later."

Then he was rearing back, pushing his boxers down and

tossing them away. His cock was flushed and hard and I reached out to touch him, wanting to feel the smooth warmth of his erection under my fingertips. His cock jumped at my gentle touch and Charlie smiled.

"I have spent all night dozing off and on and wanting you," he said.

My heart did its own jump from his words.

"I want you to too" I said, squeezing again. A bit harder this time.

He looked like he wondered. Wondered if I really wanted him. That broke my heart just a little. I tried to focus on the evidence of his lust and not the possible hurt feelings on his face.

"Then I'll come get you," he said. He seemed to be content to focus on our physical union and not what was going on in our heads. That could be quite messy—the head bit.

"Come get me," I whispered.

Charlie covered me with his body and his cock rode the swollen, slick split of my pussy lips. He thrust his hips, rubbing his shaft and his cockhead along my clitoris and my slit. It only made me bite my lip and hold my breath and mentally pray for him to plunge into me. I held my words until he nudged me hard enough that I nearly came. Then I took his face in my hands, kissed him desperately and said, "Jesus, Charlie, please. Please fuck me. You're driving me nuts."

He smiled down at me and the smile spoke volumes. That had been his intention and the only thing that was setting me free were my pleas. Thank God I'd given in to them.

"Okay, Ace. I can do that." He pushed his hands beneath my ass and I spread my legs, pulling them up, opening for him as much as I possibly could. I could feel how terribly wet I was. How ready. When he began to enter me, taking his time, torturing me more, I hummed with every inch of penetration.

"You're killing me."

"I'm not killing you. I'm taking you. And I'm taking my time about it."

He was.

I was just about to beg again when he thrust hard and drove into me. The air fled my body and I shuddered beneath him. One more rough thrust and I was coming, grasping at his arms and shoulders with clutching fingers like I was drowning.

"Charlie," I said against his neck. "God, yes. Jesus..." Then I laughed at my clichéd words. They might be clichéd but they were honest.

He rocked against me, grinding his lean hips back and forth, forcing my body to take his full weight as he lay flat against me. Charlie dragged his teeth along my shoulder and then bit me gently. He arched back to get better access to my nipple, scraped it with this teeth, bit me there. It was a little less gentle and the sudden burst of pain quickly bled into a heavy thumping pleasure.

I moaned.

Charlie found my wrists with his hands and pulled them down by my hips, pinning me there. His body flush against mine, his fingers trapping my hands down by my sides. He continued to rock and to grind until my mouth popped open and words came out. A huge spill of nonsense words. Babbling. Pleas.

He kissed me silent, stifling my words. *Charlie, please, yes, good, right there...* I heard myself as if from far away as I kept talking even when the orgasm hit me. As the spasm pulled every last shard of pleasure from me. I was full of white light, I was happy, I was perfect.

He put his forehead to mine and moved faster. Now that

my pleasure had taken all my strength, Charlie aimed to take his own pleasure, and he did when he released my wrists, shoved his hands beneath my ass and angled me just so.

He only said my name once and then, on a kiss, he surrendered to his release. His body going taut, his heart banging so hard I felt its thumping against my own chest.

The world came back into focus a minute later. The tick of the clock, the sounds of people outside, trucks and airplanes and the chatter of the upstairs neighbor's TV.

Charlie looked down at me, smoothed my hair back. He looked intense. He looked serious. It worried me how he looked. My chest crimped with worry. "So tell me," he said.

"Tell you what?"

"Why'd you hit her?"

"Because she was being an asshole," I said, honestly.

"Yeah, she was. But you were pretty much done. At least it seemed like it. But then she said the toddler thing. And the boyfriend thing. So which set you off?"

I stared down at him. He'd moved to lay his head on my belly. His blue eyes were so honest. They were the kind of eyes you never wanted to see sad. Especially if it was your fault.

But I was honest. "I don't know, Charlie. I just reacted."

I sighed, smoothed his hair down with my fingertips. His eyes drifted shut so I did it again. I could see by his face that it felt good.

"Can't we just leave things the way they are? Can't we just be happy right here?"

"With the eating and the movies and the fucking," he said. It wasn't a question. "And the occasional disastrous outing with dear friends," he added.

I chuckled. "Boy, you hit that nail on the head."

"But to answer your question," he went on. I felt my

body brace. I could feel that something was coming. Some words that had the potential to change it all. "I am okay with things the way they are now. I am okay with the let's-not-name-what-we-have game." He looked up at me, his eyes so honest my throat felt tight with emotion. "But not forever. I can't even promise for long."

He reared up on his elbows and watched me as he said it. "You make me happy, Abby. No matter what anyone else says or thinks or feels about it. You. Make. Me. *Happy*. So I'm not going to be content with you being the girl I'm fucking for a very long time."

"Girl," I snorted. But it was a defense mechanism. I could hear it in my voice.

He grabbed my hand. Kissed my knuckles. "Fine. Woman. Whatever you want to call it, it won't work forever. Because I am very swiftly falling for you. And I refuse to stifle that. Got it?"

I opened my mouth and the doorbell rang. We both froze and then laughed. But he wouldn't let me move to answer it until I answered him. "I've got it," I said. Then I hurried to the foyer.

I looked through the lace covered window and my face and toes went numb. The visitors waved. I held up a finger. "Just a minute!" I yelled but my whole body had gone tingly.

I rushed into the bedroom and hissed to Charlie, "Hurry! Get dressed! Get dressed!"

Charlie looked up, startled. But he began to pull his jeans on and found his shirt. "Why? What's wrong?"

I dropped to the edge of the bed even as the doorbell bonged again. That would be Heath. My playful kid. "It's my kids," I groaned.

Sommer Marsden

CHAPTER SEVENTEEN

"Coming!" I yelled. I heard Charlie take a deep breath. He was as nervous as I was. I tried to remember that.

I threw the door open and tried to be pleasantly surprised. Maternal. I tried to be happy to see them despite the fact that my heart was racing. We'd been having a fairly heavy conversation and I was positive I reeked of sex.

I felt woozy at the thought.

I accepted a hug from both of them, though a little stiffer than normal. I kissed them both and said somewhat convincingly, "Come in guys. What are you doing here? I thought…"

Heath held two big pizza boxes and Rose a twelve pack of soda.

"We came to have a linner with you," Heath said. His eyes were sparkly with mischief. My predicament amused him.

"Linner?" Charlie said from the background. He was standing in the doorway that led from foyer to dining room.

"Lunch and dinner combined," Rose said, nodding. "Hi. I'm Rose."

I inhaled deeply. "Jeesh. Sorry. Charlie, this is my daughter Rose and my son Heath. They are supposed to be back at school and base in that order."

"I spent the night with Debbie last night," Rose said.

"I visited Keith and Bob. We played pool. I'm not late until seven tonight, Mom. We figured we'd see you one more time." He laughed and pushed past me and Charlie into the dining room. I followed.

"We thought you might miss us, mother," Rose said. She was playing with me and I felt my cheeks color.

"Of course I miss you!"

"And," Heath said, "We took a shot that maybe we'd get to meet Charlie if we just stopped in."

Charlie chuckled, looked away. He wasn't going to help me here.

"I said I'd set it up…soon…but…" I really didn't know what to say.

"How long's it been?" Rose shot past me and went to grab plates in the kitchen. "Over a month?"

"Roughly," Charlie said.

I shot him a look and he shrugged as if to say *Hey, she asked…*

"After twenty years and then a divorce I think roughly a steady month of dating warrants dinner with us." Rose set the table.

"Or linner," Heath piped in.

I sighed. "Okay, but a little notice—"

"Would only give you a chance to wiggle out of it," she said. "So, mother," Rose said, plopping a piece of pizza on each plate while her twin brother poured out soda. "Tell us about this fist fight you had last night."

Then Charlie sat down, laughing outright, he bit into his

pizza and said, "You know, Ace, I like your kids. A lot."

I groaned, flopping down in a chair. When I stared at the pizza my stomach rumbled. Rose patted my hand. "Surrender to the process, mom."

"It wasn't a fist fight," I said.

"Oh, but it was," Charlie said. I tried to kick him under the table but he dodged me. Laughing.

That was good, right? Laughing with my kids. But part of me felt a bright, sharp stab of fear.

"So tell us," Heath said, hunkering down.

"Traitors," I said in general.

"Spill," Heath said, but he was addressing Charlie, not me.

I watched, mesmerized, as Charlie told the story, managing to make it funny. Managing to make me seem somewhat heroic instead of inebriated. And he even made it child-friendly. Not that my children were *children* per se, but I was their mother and didn't want to look like a fist wielding lush to them. Charlie pulled that off.

When the pizza was gone and Rose was subtly eyeing her watch as if to signal her brother she had to get on the road, I found myself wishing it didn't have to end. It had been good. It had been comfortable, of all things.

"I have to get Cinderella up to Frostburg before she turns into a pumpkin. Then I have to high tail it to base," Heath said. He stood, leaned across the table to kiss me. "Thanks for letting us bring you linner, Ma."

I snorted with faux outrage.

"Nice to meet you, man," Heath said, shaking Charlie's hand.

It went like that. A nice normal goodbye that included Charlie. There was ease. There was calm. I had raised my children to be nonjudgmental, inclusive and kind. I'd done a good job, I realized, tears pricking my eyes as they waved from the doorway and then were gone.

Charlie turned to me and I couldn't stop myself. I wrapped my arms around his neck and kissed him. "Wow," I said. "Wow! That went well."

"It did."

"It was so easy!" I marveled.

"It was."

I kissed him again but noted a tightness to his mouth. A hesitancy in his lips.

I pulled back to study his face. "What's wrong?"

Charlie shrugged. "After that, I realize, the only thing standing in our way is you."

"I—"

"They accepted me wholeheartedly."

"They did," I said.

"I thought you were holding back with me—holding back your emotions—because of your kids. But it's not them, Abby."

My heart dropped like a stone into my stomach. At least it felt that way.

"But it's not them. It's you."

"Charlie. I never lied to you. I've told you the way I feel—my worries—from day one."

He nodded. "True. But I am having more and more trouble accepting it. Maybe that's me. I'll take the blame."

"Charlie—"

"I have to go. I want you to just think—open-mindedly, please—about us. And where you are willing to go in this relationship. Please. And give me a call when you know."

I opened my mouth to say something but had no idea what to say.

He looked at me on the way out the door. "And do me a favor, stop thinking of me as a kid. Stop calling me a kid. Stop acting like I'm a child. I'm two years older than I was when my father had me. And doing the math, about three years older than you were when you had those two. Were you a child then? Would you have wanted to be treated the way you sometimes treat me?"

I shut my mouth, my eyes shiny with tears. He took pity on me and kissed me on the cheek as I stood there dumbfounded.

What the fuck had just happened?

*

It took me a stunned week of missing him to realize how much I was missing him. It took me another week of denying I was missing him before I called him. And when I called him, I whispered into the phone. Asked him to come talk, told him I'd missed seeing him. But I still admitted what was in my heart.

"I don't know if I can give you what you want, Charlie. I just don't. And..." There was total silence on the phone. Nothing but the sound of open air and held breath. "I'm afraid. Afraid I'll disappoint you. Or worse, myself."

"I'll come over tonight," he said. "We'll talk." Then: "Listen, I know it's fast. Even I can see that. But Abby, I can't deny how I feel. And I refuse to be a person who puts my life on hold because I talk myself out of things. Especially good things. Important things."

The thought of seeing him made my blood jump in my veins. Made my heart twist in my chest. But I wasn't sure what I was going to say—or hell, agree to—until I saw him.

I was terrified. But I knew one thing above all others. I needed to see Charlie. And I think that scared me more than anything else.

CHAPTER EIGHTEEN

"You look nice," he said when I opened the door.

I looked down as if I had no idea what I was wearing. I was still dressed in the work clothes I'd been in all day. A gray and black print wrap dress, hose, and black heels. I hadn't even kicked those off yet. "Oh, thanks. I'm still dressed for w—"

That was as far as I got. He was in, kicking the door shut, taking me in his arms. Charlie pressed his lips to mine, kissed me softly. When I responded, we both groaned and he cradled the back of my head in his hands, kissing me more deeply. His tongue swept along mine and he gently nipped the tip of my tongue with his teeth. I felt that sparkle of pain in my belly and lower.

"Charlie, I—"

"Shut up, shut up," he said, raspy. He was laughing and I smiled to hear it. "We can talk…later. First…" He picked me up in his arms and carried me toward the bedroom. I wrapped my legs around his waist. I had forgotten how tall he was. How strong.

I was wet, I could feel it beneath my panties. The soaked

split of my sex as it pressed to my underthings which then pressed to my dress which then pressed to him.

"Too many layers between us," I murmured around another kiss. I hadn't meant to say it aloud but he nodded and growled. "I agree."

When I hit the bed he was on me. His intensity stole my breath. Charlie pulled the tie on my dress and parted it. He opened the dress like he was opening a gift and when he exposed me in my bra and panties and thigh high hose, I could see my heart jumping when I looked at my chest.

He touched me there. Right where the skin above my heart danced. Somehow that touch was a thousand times more seductive than if he'd pulled down my bra cups or yanked off my knickers.

"Charlie…" I started and then petered off. Because I had no idea at all what to say. Or what I *should* say.

"Shh…" he said. He bent and placed his lips on that skin. The necklace he'd given me slid to the side, warm against my skin. He kissed the place where my heart staggered in my chest at having him so close.

I tugged at his shirt, his belt, his jean loops, anything I could reach. But he never let me get much purchase. He simply moved away from me and kept kissing me. His lips drifted from above my heart to my collar bone, to my shoulder, to my throat. He dragged his teeth along the pulse that slammed in my neck and then kissed tenderly along my jawline. All the while I shivered and grasped at him. All the while I pulled at him, wanting him inside me.

He opened my bra with the front clasp. When the cups fell to the sides he outlined the tip of each nipple with his rigid tongue. He sucked each one in turn until my cunt flexed wetly, wanting…needing.

"You know I missed you so fucking much. Your laugh…" Charlie said. He kissed his way down my belly and I watched the muscles flutter even as I felt the flex and dance of them beneath his ministrations. "Your body."

He hooked his fingers in the sides of my panties and tugged them down. Charlie moaned when he looked at me and the sensation of his eyes on me warmed me head to toe. He tossed my panties on the floor and parted my thighs. His breath was warm and invasive as he studied me and said, "I missed your body, Ace," he said. 'Touching it…"

Charlie dragged his fingers along my outer lips and then thumbed my clitoris firmly so that I wiggled beneath his touch. "Tasting it…" He parted his lips and sucked at me, licked me, ate me like I was his favorite flavor.

I came with a burst of sound and bright lights behind my closed eyelids. It only took a few minutes. Just a few minutes of him touching me and licking me and being close to me. That was all that was needed for me to surrender to pleasure.

My hands battled his for an instant for his belt buckle but he batted them away. He was bare in what felt like a year's time and the blink of an eye simultaneously. I sat up fast, bending to take him in hand and then into my mouth. I licked the solid, silken length of him and sucked the tip of his cock. Charlie groaned, shook his head, and pushed me back with tented fingers.

I gasped, laughing at his rudeness. He shook his head again. "Later, Ace. You can do that later. I want you to do that later. But now…"

He nudged my legs wide, shoved his hands beneath my hips and hiked them up so he could enter me while remaining fairly upright to watch. His eyes stayed glued to where our bodies met. Where he penetrated me and we became joined.

"Fuck." He exhaled the word on a breath and seemed content to study where he thrust into me. I arched up, moving to take him, driving my hips up so that every time he plunged deep his body grazed my swollen clit.

"I missed you," I said. It was supposed to be a simple declaration of happiness. Instead, I felt tears sting at my eyes. My throat grew thick with emotion. I blinked and swallowed, willing it all away.

He caught the look, let go of my hips and folded himself over me, pressed down on me. We were chest to chest, hip to hip, belly to belly…eye to eye.

"I missed you too, Abby. More than I can possibly express." He kissed me, his mouth soft at first and then more insistent.

Charlie moved his hips in small circles, dragged them from side to side, torturing us both until neither could stand it anymore.

"Jesus. Charlie. Please." Three short puffs of air.

He nodded once. "Yeah, me too," he said. Then his rhythm picked up, his hips moving surely and forcefully, I wrapped my legs around his lean waist, held him as close as I possibly could and focused on the feel of him moving in me and the feel of his mouth on my skin. His teeth found my pulse point and he bit me.

I came, clutching at his shoulders and saying his name. He was right behind me. He simply said, "Ace. Christ, how I missed you." Then he pulled free, flipped me on my belly.

I put my hips up, my forehead to the bed. He entered me from behind, fast, gripping my hair in his fist to hold me beneath him. I'd missed him. This intimacy. And when, after a few short, brutal thrusts, he came, I had to wipe at my wet eyes with my fingers.

*

"We got the makeup sex out of the way," I said, propping myself up on the headboard. We sipped wine and he watched me. I blushed beneath his gaze because every time he looked at me it reminded me of a hungry man looking at his first meal in days.

"Is that how you look at it?" He sat cross legged, nursing his wine, watching me.

"No. Not really. I was trying to be funny. Break the ice. You know."

He touched my calf, rubbing it so that the knots I didn't even know were there began to loosen. "That's not funny. Not to me."

"Sorry," I whispered. "Not to me, either. Not really."

"What are we going to do?"

"Can't we—"

"Can't we go on as it is? Nope." He shook his head and he looked sad. "I don't think so. I don't think you get it, Abby. I think I love you. If you hadn't pushed me away for two weeks I'd probably know."

"You think?" I asked, my heart falling, my head dizzy.

He shrugged, looked away embarrassed. "I've never been in love before, to tell the truth. But all the things I've thought love are...this is it."

My lips had gone numb. "Charlie—"

"Do you want to break up? Or stop...this? Whatever you want to call it."

"Are those my options? This or no this?"

"You don't have to love me," he said, softly. "But you have to be more to me than the girl I'm fucking. That means something to me."

I licked my lips. "Charlie, what does that mean?"

"At the very least you have to be my girl, Abby." He said it with an adorable smirk. I had to fight the urge to crawl into his lap and kiss him.

"I'm scared," I said again. "I just got out of a long marriage. Long. As in almost half my life, Charlie. And now you want me to rush—"

"Nope. I do not want you to rush. I want you to *consider*. Which you are not doing. If you're honest. You're not, are you?"

I shook my head, compelled to be honest. "Not really. No."

"Why?"

"I feel like I'm not ready."

"All of you?"

I chewed my lip. Remembering my heart. How I felt when I knew he was coming to see me. When he touched me. When he told me how he felt.

"Not all of me," I admitted.

He nodded. "That's what I thought. I want you to do something for me." He moved to his knees, set the wine glass on the nightstand and put his hands in my hair. One gentle kiss and then: "Will you?"

"What is it?"

"The weather is changing. Not quite nice but we have days here and there where it's spring-like. Come away with me. Next week. Seven days, me and you."

"Take off work?" I said it incredulously. Which made me sad. Had I become that person? The workaholic who used her job to avoid having a life?

"If you can. Do you have time?"

I thought of the over three and a half weeks I had accrued. I had to take less time now that the kids were grown and gone. No more sick kid days and I rarely allowed myself to stay home unless I was fairly ill. "I do."

"Then come with me." He dropped to his side and pulled me in against him. Wrapping me in his arms. I felt him breathing. It was soothing so I shut my eyes.

"That's a big step," I said.

"Maybe. But it's what I want. A step. From you. I can't deny how I feel about you. How it grows a little more every day, but I can't torture myself either."

I sighed. I understood, but I was so scared.

"Come away with me, Ace."

"What will we do?" I asked, feeling slightly anxious. Then I realized how stupid that sounded and laughed.

Charlie laughed too, but he smoothed my hair back as if he felt my worry. "We'll be together. Uninterrupted time. Some wine, fires, hiking on the days we don't need fires and the sun is out. Maybe some lingerie." He patted my ass and I laughed. "I'll cook for you. Outside some days like a caveman. We can just be together and you can decide."

"Decide what?" I asked but I knew. And it was audible in my voice so he knew I knew.

"If you can be more to me than just someone to sleep with. If you can take that next step and be my girl."

I wanted to cry but refused.

"Will you?" he asked, brushing away a tear. "Come away with me for the week. Give me a chance. Give *us* a chance."

I nodded. "Okay. I'll go."

He pushed me back and kissed me. And then it was happening all over again. Us, together. No talking, bodies moving, soft cries. I was absolutely terrified of going, but

Charlie had taken a piece of my heart. He meant so much to me. More than I'd ever want to admit. I had to do this to be fair. To give us that chance.

I shut my eyes and pushed away all the thoughts of the future. I focused on the here and the now and the feel of his body pressed up against mine and his lips soft on my lips.

Stay tuned for book 2 in The Accidental Trilogy:
The Accidental Girlfriend

If you liked this you might like **Angry Sex**

Luna Watkins can't remember feeling so stressed. Her teenage son Nick's health issues are reemerging and her ex Ben wants to help but is just making ends meet with odd jobs. Her catering business is thriving but too hectic for her to handle, at least that's what it feels like. Not to mention since she's been divorced, she hasn't dated much and has had sex even less. When Nick decides to visit his grandparents for the summer, Luna is devastated. And yet, she sees a chance to work through her anger and her angst. Maybe some time to feed her body, mind and soul knowing he's well taken care of.

Enter Adam Singleton, her new, last minute server. Handsome, gruff Adam who's working through his own anger. Flirting turns to sparring. Sparring turns to angry sex—like therapy but naked. As time goes by and Luna and Adam become even more entangled, with their hardships and each other, the question becomes, does angry sex turn to more anger…or peace?

COMING SOON from Excessica

Crossroads

Wesley Moore bargains with a demon to find success. The price seems cheap when he's alone and his family has a history of early deaths. What he doesn't count on is falling in love with two different people just before his deal comes due. Can Wesley come away with his life and both the boy and the girl?

ABOUT THE AUTHOR

Professional dirty word writer, gluten free baker, sock addict, fat wiener dog walker, expert procrastinator. Called "one of the top storytellers in the erotic genre" by Violet Blue, Sommer Marsden writes for HarperCollins Mischief, Ellora's Cave, Excessica, Xcite Books and Resplendence Publishing. She's the author of numerous erotic novels including Lost in You, Restricted Release, Boys Next Door, Restless Spirit, and Learning to Drown.

Visit http://sommermarsden.blogspot.com

YOU'VE REACHED

"THE END!"

BUY THIS AND MORE TITLES AT
www.eXcessica.com

eXcessica's YAHOO GROUP
groups.yahoo.com/group/eXcessica/

eXcessica's FORUM
www.eXcessica.com/forum

Check us out for updates about eXcessica books!